KT-559-328

Renew by phone or online

1804571661

SPECIAL MESSAGE TO READERS

This book is published under the auspices of

THE ULVERSCROFT FOUNDATION

(registered charity No. 264873 UK)

Established in 1972 to provide funds for research, diagnosis and treatment of eye diseases. Examples of contributions made are: —

A Children's Assessment Unit at
Moorfield's Hospital, London.

•

Twin operating theatres at the
Western Ophthalmic Hospital, London.

•

A Chair of Ophthalmology at the
Royal Australian College of Ophthalmologists.

•

The Ulverscroft Children's Eye Unit at the
Great Ormond Street Hospital For Sick Children,
London.

You can help further the work of the Foundation by making a donation or leaving a legacy. Every contribution, no matter how small, is received with gratitude. Please write for details to:

**THE ULVERSCROFT FOUNDATION,
The Green, Bradgate Road, Anstey,
Leicester LE7 7FU, England.
Telephone: (0116) 236 4325**

**In Australia write to:
THE ULVERSCROFT FOUNDATION,
c/o The Royal Australian and New Zealand
College of Ophthalmologists,
94-98, Chalmers Street, Surry Hills,
N.S.W. 2010, Australia**

CATFOOT

He had nothing on the guy — no name, no physical description, he didn't even know what crime he was guilty of! But Jim Catfoot, agent with the Pinkerton Detective Agency, knew that something was wrong. He'd got some questions he wanted answering. Mule-headed and using the few clues that he'd scraped together, he set about his task, unaware that this mission would put him on a countrywide chase — a chase that could only end in violent confrontation . . .

J. WILLIAM ALLEN

CATFOOT

Complete and Unabridged

LINFORD
Leicester

First published in Great Britain in 2007 by
Robert Hale Limited
London

First Linford Edition
published 2008
by arrangement with
Robert Hale Limited
London

The moral right of the author has been asserted

Copyright © 2007 by J. William Allen
All rights reserved

British Library CIP Data

Allen, J. William
    Catfoot.—Large print ed.—
Linford western library
    1. Western stories
    2. Large type books
    I. Title
    823.9′2 [F]

    ISBN 978–1–84782–278–9

Published by
F. A. Thorpe (Publishing)
Anstey, Leicestershire

Set by Words & Graphics Ltd.
Anstey, Leicestershire
Printed and bound in Great Britain by
T. J. International Ltd., Padstow, Cornwall

This book is printed on acid-free paper

For Lewis Maitland Holmes

1

And thus it was written that some shall die by pestilence, some by the plague, and that some poor bastard is going to get it out of a .45.

The poor bastard in question was dressed in a black uniform with gold braid on his lapels and cuffs. At least he was well dressed when he met his maker.

A train guard, the poor fellow hadn't intended going for the Winchester on the wall rack, but it was the first time he'd faced gunmen, and dizziness had started to come over him the moment they leapt up into the bullion car. Then, when he found himself looking down the wrong end of revolver barrels, his legs seemed to disappear beneath him. Overcome, he'd staggered to the side of the car with his hand outstretched for support, unwittingly towards the wall — the wall on which the Winchester was lodged — the action that had prompted the shooting. And now he was dead meat on the wooden boards.

Dick Bodeen glowered at his companion and the smoking gun in his fist. 'What the hell did you do that for, you bozo?'

'He was going for one of the guns on the rack, boss.'

'Was he hell! Couldn't you see his eyes? He was on the point of fainting. The guy was just falling down, you schmuck.'

Billy Boy O'Hara looked down at the dead man and hefted his gun. 'Well, I gave him good reason to fall down!'

He sniggered at his own attempt at a joke but Bodeen grunted and, using the unanticipated development to their advantage, turned to the remaining guard. 'Well, my friend, now you can see what happens if you don't cooperate — a slug between the eyes — so do yourself a favour and open that strongbox.'

With a 'Yes, sir,' the man began

fumbling with the keys.

The two robbers had employed what was fast becoming the standard method for relieving a train of its valuable freight, specifically jumping the train at an isolated refuelling stop and decoupling the bullion car. Then the engineer would be forced at gunpoint to proceed with the locomotive and remaining cars. Should there be anyone aboard the main section of the train who might give armed resistance, by the time they had been informed and the locomotive put into reverse, the desperadoes would be clear — provided they got in and out fast.

'Get a move on!' Bodeen snapped at the guard.

'It's done, sir,' the man said, swinging open the metal door.

The thieves grabbed the bundles of bills. When they'd cleaned the thing out, O'Hara pointed to a bigger box.

'Now that one,' he ordered the guard.

Bodeen raised a staying hand to the uniformed man. 'Leave it.'

3

'Eh?' O'Hara said, puzzlement contorting his features.

'No.'

'Why not, boss? It's bigger. There'll be even more in it.'

'Can't you see the name? Adams Express Company. We leave it.' One by one he took the Winchesters from the wall rack, shucked out the loads and hurled the weapons as far as he could through the open door.

'I figure you wouldn't use the guns,' he said to the apprehensive railroad man, 'but I'm just putting temptation out of your way.' He nodded to his companion. 'Now let's git.'

When O'Hara had dropped to the ground, Bodeen stood contemplatively in the doorway for a moment watching his comrade retrieve the horses. In the distance the rest of the train could be seen firing up to reverse towards them. After some seconds' thought he turned to the guard. 'Likely the authorities will figure out who we are,' he said in a

4

low voice, and he pulled down his bandanna to reveal his square features and droop moustache. 'So there's no harm in telling you. The name's Bodeen.'

It was a strange thing to do. In the circumstances of the time when a gamut of desperadoes were playing mayhem with banks and trains across the territory, it was unlikely the perpetrators of this particular job would be identified with any certainty — especially with the robbers being masked.

The guard's face paled even further. Now he knew the name and had seen the robber's face, his death had to be on the agenda.

'Dick Bodeen,' the man went on. 'So, when you tell the tale to the law and your bosses, just make sure you tell 'em that it wasn't me who put a bullet through your pal. It was the lunkhead who rides with me — him yonder — name of Billy Boy O'Hara. You got that?'

'Er, yes, sir.'

'Then say the names.'

The man falteringly repeated them.

'And which of the two did the killing of your workmate?' Bodeen insisted, aware of the fear that might be clouding the man's brain.

'Billy Boy O'Hara, sir,' the man stuttered. 'He was the one that done it.'

'OK, you got that straight?'

Bodeen waited for the man's 'yes, sir,' then he dropped through the door space. In seconds he and his accomplice were astride their horses and hightailing out of the place.

By the time that they had disappeared over a distant ridge the reversing train had come to a halt a few yards from the bullion car. Men had left the train and were hesitantly approaching. The guard who had been spared jumped down to greet them.

'They killed Fred,' he shouted. 'But I got their names. Yes, sirree, I got their names.'

★ ★ ★

At their temporary camp, Bodeen took one of the two even piles that he had meticulously counted out and handed it to his partner.

'There you are, fifty-fifty,'

'I still don't understand, boss,' O'Hara said, after he'd studied his cut before stuffing it into his pockets. 'Back there, why didn't we get the guy to open the big box? OK, we've got away with almost two grand apiece here, but there could have been — huh — another ten thousand in that box.'

'Probably was.'

'Then why didn't we take that as well?'

Bodeen stuffed his own cut into his saddle-bag. 'See, the difference between you and me, Billy Boy, is you don't think. I know it ain't your doing — 'cos the good Lord gave you nothing to think with — so let me explain. The box to which you refer had got the Adams Express brand on it. Now it's a well-known fact that the Adams Express Company has a contract with the Pinkertons.'

He looked for a reaction in his partner but got none. 'You know,' he went on, 'the Pinkerton Detective Agency down in Denver? Their headquarters might be in Chicago but they got agents all over the country, and not just out here in the west. They work hand in hand with railroad detectives. And they got an army contract which means they can bring in the army if they want to. Well, you cross them and you got them on your tail till hell freezes over. They just don't give up. Borrowed their motto from the Mounties: 'we always get our man'. And, just like the Mounties, they mean it — so we don't touch their stuff.'

He shook his head as he poured out coffee. 'I've explained to you before but it don't seem to sink in. With a *clean* heist all you got is local law after you. But their hearts ain't really in it and they soon give up. So, provided you can keep ahead of 'em for a spell, the worst the local hicks ever do is to circulate wanted posters — and them things are rarely good likenesses, so the odds are still on your side. But the Pinks, Billy Boy, they're another matter.'

He rubbed his chin as he thought about it. 'But we do have a problem. Trouble is, this job ain't been clean. You put a guy's lights out back there. So, although we ain't got the Pinks on our tail, the law's gonna put in a little extra effort into this job. And I don't have to tell you, murder makes it a Federal issue. So there's gonna be boys in several states on the lookout for us.'

'But they don't know who we are, do they, boss?'

'No, at least we got that advantage.'

Bodeen smiled inwardly at his lie, then added, 'But it means we're still gonna have to get out of the territory for a spell.'

2

It was late afternoon when Jim Catfoot entered Denver from the north. The place was big — according to the mayor's oft-repeated claim, the biggest town in the West after San Francisco. Catfoot didn't know if that was just braggadocio but he knew the place was big. When he hit the familiar main street he found himself in a milieu of wagons and buckboards. Yeah, the place was sure big. And still growing.

As he negotiated his way through the traffic, folk looked with passing interest at the horse that he hauled in his wake. What caught their curiosity was the fact that its rider was handcuffed.

Catfoot pulled up outside the law office, thumped to the ground and hitched the horses. His prisoner offered no resistance as Catfoot got him down and ushered him through the doorway.

'Got a present for you, Frank.'

The lawman threw a welcoming smile. 'Well, I'll be! Outside of Tom Horn, if it ain't the agency's principal dog-catcher west of Chicago.'

'Tom who?' Catfoot grunted in mock affront. He was aware of the name but didn't see the connection.

'Didn't you know, Jim? Your guys have got the great Tom Horn chasing horse thieves down near the border.'

'Huh, makes a change from the law chasing him. Mind, they say there's advantage in turning a poacher into a gamekeeper.'

The lawman eyed the cuffed man. 'And what's this critter been up to?'

'Fraud case,' the 'dog-catcher' explained. 'Managed to get clear with a nice piece of change belonging to his employer back in New York. Seems he reckoned that once he'd crossed a few state and territorial lines he'd be safe.'

'But didn't figure on the long arm of the Pinkertons, eh?'

'Right. Anyways, Frank, as the bozo's

got to be shipped back east, the company's gonna have to ask you to hold him while extradition is cleared.' He shrugged and added, 'But don't know how long that will take.'

'No problem, Jim.'

'OK, I'll bring the necessary papers over when I've reported to the office.'

'He give you any trouble?'

Catfoot dropped his backside on the desk and gestured to his prisoner's dusty suit. 'No. Dressed like a dude and talking Eastern, he wasn't difficult to locate. And, as for being a villain, he don't know which end is up. Gave in as meek as a mouse when I confronted him.' He patted the butt of his Army Colt. 'Didn't even have to use this baby. Wished all cases were as easy.'

'Coffee, Jim?' the lawman offered, once the prisoner was behind bars. 'You look like you need it.'

'No thanks, Frank. They'll be waiting on me over at the office — then I've got some catching up to do with my missus.'

'You got some understanding woman there, Jim. Not to mention one helluva good-looker.'

Catfoot winked as he headed for the street. 'I know — that's why I'm taking a rain check on the coffee.'

★ ★ ★

The door had an eye painted on it: 'The Eye That Never Sleeps'. It was a copy of the large sign that adorned the office of the agency's Western headquarters back in Chicago. Catfoot pushed through and made his report to the superintendent.

'You done a fine job on this, Jim,' his boss said in conclusion. 'This'll keep us in good with Chicago and, more important, head office in New York.'

The Pinkerton Agency thrived on publicity. Success — especially in a case like this in which the chase had stretched across the whole country — was not only good for drumming up new business, but it made the job of its agents easier by prompting villains to think twice before making an assault on the assets of the company's clients.

The manager opened up a ledger and studiously made an entry. 'I'll wire New York with the news and get 'em to start extradition proceedings.'

He perused the figures before closing the book. 'You got some free time due, Jim. And you earned it. You been on this case a month of Sundays.' He took the stub of a pencil from his desk and crossed to a calendar on the wall. After a few seconds' contemplation he drew an oval around a week and tapped his pencil against the mark. 'Report back in seven days.'

Catfoot nodded. 'I could sure do with it.' Then he gestured back to the door with his thumb. 'By the way, Frank's needing documentation for his records over at the law office.'

'You've done enough, Jim. Leave that with me.' He nodded at the calendar. 'Now I don't want to see your hide in here for seven clear days. You got that, mister?'

With an eager 'Thank you, sir,' Catfoot saluted and headed for the door.

Outside he paused on the sidewalk and breathed deep as he looked up and down the bustling thoroughfare. There was always satisfaction in bringing a case to a close. He was weary, but the sun was shining and life was good. He had a job he liked, one that pulled good money, more than cow punching at least, and a good woman waiting for him at home.

It had always been his habit to take back a present after a long absence. So, after he had settled his horse in at the livery, he toured the stores until he found an attractive bonnet in pink, Flo's favourite colour. Whistling, he made his way down the alley to the door that led to their apartment.

The landlady's thirteen-year-old daughter was sitting on the stoop.

'Hi there, Lucy,' he said, smoothing

her hair as he passed.

'Howdy, Mr Catfoot.' He might have detected a little apprehension in her voice as she replied but, if he did, he dismissed it and resumed his whistling as he bounded up the stairs. But his whistling stopped when he flung open the door to be greeted by bare boards. He stood transfixed for some seconds, then dropped on a chair to read the note he discovered on the table.

'Jim,' it read. 'It's over. Don't come after me. Do me one last favour and just sign the divorce papers when they come through.'

'Jeez,' he breathed. He turned the note over. Nothing on the back. He glanced around the room. The furniture that went with the apartment was still there, but no sign of Flo's ornaments. Dazed, he rose and moseyed around the place. The wardrobe door was hanging open; Flo's clothes gone.

He clumped downstairs and knocked on the door. It was opened by a serious-faced, elderly woman.

'You know?' she faltered.

'Yes. I've been up there. When . . . ?'

'About a week back.'

'By herself?'

The woman hesitated, then added, 'No, with a feller.' She touched his arm. 'I'm real sorry, Jim. I thought you were so happy together.'

'Yeah,' he grunted. He remained silent for a spell, then said, 'This feller, somebody I know?'

'I think maybe so. Adey Cooke.'

Yeah, he knew him. The fellow ran a dry goods store. Catfoot had played horseshoes with him on Sunday afternoons a few times; and cards for dimes in the saloon. Regular guy. Straight, that is until now, the bastard.

'I was so worried,' the woman continued. 'I guessed something was going on. Saw him about the place a lot. Then I knew trouble was really brewing when he started staying over for the night. They tried to hide it from me but I knew. Then, some nights Mrs Catfoot wouldn't come back here. I

17

guess on those nights they stayed over at his place.'

'You know where they're at?'

'No. But all the signs are they've left town.'

'Left town? He was an established member of the community.'

'Well, it's clear he's sold his business as there's a new sign over it. There's a fresh face behind the counter too.'

'You know where they've gone?'

'No.'

He sighed. 'Well, thanks, Mrs Brook.'

'If there's anything I can do, you only have to ask.'

'Yeah, thanks.'

Back in the apartment he dropped on the bed and stared at the ceiling. Suppose it had to happen, he told himself. Just hadn't seen it coming was all. It was his being away for great chunks of time that had done it. From time to time Flo had kicked against the long absences necessitated by his job but he hadn't thought she was serious. Maybe she hadn't been serious at first.

Maybe it was her being at a loose end and allowing herself what she would have thought of as nothing more than the harmless company of a mutual friend.

And that had allowed Adey to make his play for her. Handsome Adey with his three-piece suits and clean finger-nails. How long had the critter been working up to this? He'd certainly hidden his intentions — the two-faced jasper. If only Catfoot could get his hands on him, he'd do something to that handsome face.

His stomach tight with a confusion of agitation and not knowing what to do, he rose and went to the window. He gazed blankly at the street until he caught sight of Adey's old store and he dropped back on the bed to study the ceiling again, as though it had the answers.

Hell, he only had himself to blame. Leaving an attractive woman alone for long periods. Trouble was he'd been fiddle-footed all his life, right from his early days in California. Working beef since a kid had set the stamp. Away on the range, then on drives. It was the nature of things that ranch cowboys would be nomadic, moving on every season or two. Then he'd met Flo. In time they decided they were meant for each other and became officially engaged, fancy ring and all.

Snag was a cowboy wage wasn't very much. Even the ring had knocked a dent in his meagre savings. Like most cowboys he'd dreamt of owning his own place, but in time he began to realize it was no more than a dream and he had to face reality. The responsibility of a wife — and then that of kids if they arrived. That's when he was offered a job by the Pinkertons.

The cattle outfit for which he was riding at the time had had trouble with rustlers. It was a big outfit, big enough to have the wherewithal to call in the Pinkertons, who didn't come cheap. On the rancher's behalf he'd ridden alongside the detectives and helped in apprehending the culprits. There'd been hard riding and tracking and he'd fitted well into the agency team. Finally there'd been a little gunplay in which, again, he had notably acquitted himself. So, on the strength of his performance throughout the exercise, the Pinkertons had offered him a place as an agent.

It came at the right time, just what he wanted: a good regular salary but still allowing him to spend time in the saddle out in the open with the wind blowing through his hair. His former boss had understood — he even provided the ranch as a venue for their wedding — and they'd parted amicably, with his boss telling him there was always a job available back at the ranch if things at the agency didn't work out. And the happy couple had moved into Mrs Brook's apartment in town.

Catfoot was proud of the way he had taken to his new job. Over the couple of years he'd been in the employ of the Pinkertons he'd developed his skills in detective work and the assurance to face up to lawbreakers, proving himself with a string of successful assignments.

More, the sort of life suited him. OK, sometimes he didn't see his wife for a month at a stretch but, when he did, the couple had always picked up again. It never occurred to him that one day they wouldn't, so he hadn't worried about it. Complacency he figured was the word for it. Some things you don't fret about until it's too late.

How long he lay transfixed on the bed, staring at the ceiling mulling over these thoughts, he didn't know. What he did know is that when he eventually turned his head he caught Flo's perfume in the pillow. He remembered her touch, the laughs, the good times they had had, the voice as sweet as molasses. And her cooking — boy, was she a cook.

He pictured storekeeper Adey now at her side, enjoying all these things; and anger towards the man welled up inside him again.

He swung his feet to the floor and

stared at the boards. OK, the two had left town with no forwarding address — but they wouldn't have left without being seen by somebody. Hell, he knew almost everybody in town. A little questioning would soon throw up answers and he could get on their trail. Huh, he'd tracked down enough no-goods — no-goods bent on hiding their tracks; it would be a breeze tailing a couple of inexperienced runaways.

But when he found them — then what? It wouldn't be like cornering some owlhoots. OK, he could knock the living daylights out of the snake-in-the-grass. That would give him some satisfaction. But then what? He knew Flo — well enough to understand she wouldn't have taken this decision if she didn't mean it. Chances were, if he smashed Adey about a bit, it would probably make Flo even more sympathetic to her new man. At the end of the day the exercise would be a waste of time and probably stretch out his heartbreak.

He picked up the bonnet purchased as a homecoming present and stared at it. For a moment longer, he pondered on setting out to follow them then handing Flo the bonnet in some histrionic manner and hightailing it out without another word. Some kind of stoic gesture. Then he thought: Hell, how stupid could you get?

And he decided on what to do. He clumped downstairs and dropped the hat on the young girl's head. 'There, Lucy, that's for Sunday best.' He stepped back and appraised the effect. 'Hey, makes you look even purtier.'

Then he went to the saloon and bought himself a bottle of Pogue's best.

★   ★   ★

Next morning he came to around ten o'clock with a head that felt like a steer had stomped on it. He forwent breakfast and restricted his intake to sinking a couple of cups of black coffee. That, plus soaking off the trail dust in a hot tub and shaving the stubble from his cheeks, maybe led to a ten per cent improvement in his demeanour.

Come noon, with the best part of a pot of coffee inside him, he stepped cautiously into the blinding sunlight and made his way down the street to the door with the large eye painted on it.

'I thought we'd agreed that you were on vacation,' the superintendent remarked as Catfoot entered his office.

'Been thinking about that, sir. Don't feel in the mood for taking it easy.'

The superintendent let out a low 'mmm' and said, 'Heard tell of a guy getting drunker than a skunk last night. Must say, doesn't sound like any feller I know. Guess he had his reasons.'

'Yeah,' Catfoot said. 'He had his reasons.' He dropped into a chair and pointed to the papers on his boss's desk. 'You got any new assignments there?'

'For you?'

'Yeah.'

'I don't understand, Jim.'

'Let's say I got itchy feet, sir.'

The superintendent pulled a wry face and picked up a telegram. 'Well, if your mind's fixed on keeping busy, you could maybe give Ted Faulkner a hand. Looks like there's a range war brewing down in Wright County. Their law department are paying us to provide some backup. Not much more than showing the flag. I figure that once the parties involved in the fracas are aware that Pinkertons have been called in, they'll know it's serious and will pull their horns.'

'Just what I need, sir. Give me details.'

★ ★ ★

Over in the livery where the agency quartered its horses he looked over the choice available. He needed a fresh one while his regular mount took a well-earned rest. Having paid his dues as wrangler and bronc-breaker in his early days, he knew his horses. Many folks, even some riders, didn't realize that horses didn't see food as a reward which was why there were no carrots or lumps of sugar from him. They were grazing animals, not predators. He knew their basic needs; they were social animals, their main requirement being the need to feel part of a herd. That's all. And that meant that when you were riding, the herd was just *two*: you and him. The upshot was as long as you gave him security and sociability, you'd have a trustworthy animal. And you didn't need to soft-soap him with carrots and lumps of sugar all the time. The reality was you didn't use a horse, you worked *with* him.

After a few minutes of expert appraisal he'd picked out a good one. And, a quarter hour later, the twosome herd were heading south for Wright County.

3

It was a month on. Bodeen and Billy Boy O'Hara had ridden south until the boss had figured they'd got enough territorial borders behind them. Then he had lined up their next job: the bank in a little place called Ogden.

For several days the two men rode separately into the town to case the place and learn the routine, then back in camp they pooled their knowledge. The job had several things going for it. Bank and law office were at opposite ends of town. The bank was staffed by three: the manager, an assistant and a female teller. The woman was part-time and left at noon. That left two staff. Then, just before closing, the assistant was in the habit of personally collecting the day's takings from the Mercantile. The store was run by an old woman who was unsteady on her legs and had an arrangement for the cash to be collected at the end of the day by the bank's number two to save her trouble.

There was only one reservation to the caper and that was voiced by O'Hara. 'That bank in Ogden,' he said one evening as the two took their meal around the campfire, 'I noticed that it's got one of them Pinkerton plaques on the wall.'

'I didn't know you could read,' Bodeen grunted with a chuckle.

'But, boss, you told me the Pinks meant trouble and we shouldn't touch anything they're involved in.'

'As a general rule that's so, my friend. But not all the time. This is a special case. Don't worry about it.'

'I don't understand.'

'You don't have to. I've told you: leave the thinking to me.'

★   ★   ★

Two days later they put the plan into operation. Just before closing, they took over the Mercantile, bound and gagged the old woman and waited for the bank employee to call for the takings. He was given the same treatment, and the two desperadoes made for the bank. They eased into the premises just before the manager put up the CLOSED sign.

Although the town was small, the bank held the resources of local mining companies, so it was a good take. Everything went smoothly and minutes later they slipped out of town virtually unnoticed, leaving the bank empty of funds and its tied-up manager writhing on the floor.

★ ★ ★

' 'Don't look a gift horse in the mouth,' the old man used to say.' Although he was alone, Tucker Williams enunciated the words quite loudly. He looked around the open plain to confirm yet again that he had the world to himself.

Then he took stock of the lone sorrel grazing unconcernedly before him and mused to himself some more. 'The old bastard was wrong about most things but I figure he was right on that one.'

That last thought caused him to chuckle as he cautiously approached the animal.

'Yeah, just about the only worthwhile thing the old pissant ever said in his whole goddamn life.'

The horse remained undisturbed as he neared.

'Come on, my beauty,' he said, as he patted the animal's neck and cast his eyes around the wilderness to check again that there was still no one about. 'Good stock,' he said as he appraised his find. 'Good saddle, too.'

He continued stroking and patting the creature for a while, then took the reins and walked the animal for some paces. Judging he had made friends, he mounted up. At first the horse was nervous but settled enough for Tucker to chance riding it into town.

* * *

In town he dismounted outside Ogden's sole livery stable and walked the animal to the open door.

'You in there, Mr Harris?' he called.

The liveryman came to the door. 'Howdy, Tucker.'

'How much will you trade for this hoss, Mr Harris?'

'Hey, nice piece of horseflesh you got there, Tucker. Handsome saddle, too. The saddle included in the trade?'

'Sure thing. How much?'

'I need to give the animal a good appraisement before I make you an offer. I'll tell you what: you take it into the corral while I tidy up the job that I'm working on. Won't take long.'

Tucker headed for the corral while the liveryman returned indoors where he gestured to his helpmate son to come close. 'Leave by the back door,' he whispered, 'and get your hide over to Sheriff Parrish. Tell him young Tucker Williams' brung a quality horse in for sale. Mighty suspicious. Hell, the Williams bunch ain't got a red cent between them. Got a brand on it too. All mighty suspicious. Meanwhiles, I'll stall the lad as long as I can.'

As his son left, he clattered about for a few minutes feigning useful activity. Then he picked up a rag, rubbing his hands with it as he stepped casually back into the sunshine. 'Now let's have a look-see at the merchandise,' he said loudly to the eagerly waiting young man.

Taking his time, he started with the teeth, then checked the fetlocks. Minutes into his examination a voice boomed from the corral rail.

'Where'd you get the hoss, Tucker?'

The two men turned to see the sheriff clambering over the fence.

'It's mine, Sheriff,' the young man said.

'OK, it's yours — but I still want to know how you came by it.'

'Found it,' Tucker stuttered.

'You're old enough to know finders ain't keepers — especially as far as a saddle-horse is concerned. Even more so when it's got a brand on it.'

'But, Sheriff . . .'

'Count yourself lucky, young 'un. There's some parts out here where you'd get strung up for hoss rustling.'

'I ain't rustled nothing. I told you: I found it.'

The sheriff looked the animal over. At first, following the bank job, it had seemed that no one had seen the strangers come and go. But intensive questioning around town had unearthed various snippets which he had managed to put together to get some kind of picture. It transpired that the two men had been coming into town for a few days, keeping themselves to themselves, but they had been seen.

When he had finished making his own examination of the horse, the sheriff turned to the liveryman. 'This animal fits the description of one of the bank robbers' horses. I'm impounding the critter while I get witnesses to take a look at it.' Then to the young man: 'Now tell me exactly where you found it, Tucker.'

* ★ ★

The following morning, yet another resident of Ogden thought he'd hit lucky. As was her habit, Lee Roberts's mother had sent him to catch fish but when he got to his usual spot he could see that the swelling of the river by recent rains had killed the chance of fishing. He knew that when he returned home empty-handed his ma would give him a tongue-lashing; but he sought compensation in the notion that she might let him have the gun in the hope of going hunting. Larder stocks were low and they certainly needed something for the table.

Forever deriding him as a simpleton, she hadn't allowed a gun in his hand since the time he came near to shooting his brother's head off while idly fondling the family carbine. Wasn't his fault he was clumsy. Anyways, didn't know it was loaded, did he? 'Clumsy in the head as well as the hand,' his ma always said.

So, he gave up on the river. He'd slung the rod over his shoulder and was heading home along the river in anticipation of his ma allowing him to get his hands on a real gun. It was then that he saw the saddle-bag in the river snagged in the branch of a tree. It was now partly submerged by the risen current and it took him a good five minutes to retrieve the thing, but the effort was worth it.

The most he thought he was getting was a good set of bags that would help appease his ma, compensating for his returning empty-handed. He didn't expect the two hundred dollars that he found inside.

He laid them out separately to dry in the sun and eased his back onto the grass. He stared at the sky, all thoughts of fish, his ma and her whiplash tongue gone. Boy, with two hundred dollars he'd show 'em he was somebody.

Once he'd settled on his intention and the bills were dried out, he stuffed them into his pocket and looked around for a place to hide the saddle-bags. Then, with them out of the way, he headed for town. Boy, was he lucky!

But his luck was to change later in the day. Once in town he'd bought himself some ritzy clothes and topped them off with the most expensive flat-brimmed hat in the store. Yeah, he'd show 'em. Too long he'd been the butt of joshing when he panhandled drinks. Empty-headed mule-ass, things like that they called him. Huh, a hell of a lot of folks thought they were better than others.

After strutting round the town in his new duds and enjoying the wide-eyed looks that he elicited from the towns-folk, he headed for the saloon.

With a nine-inch cigar between his fingers, he was on his second bottle of rye when the sheriff materialized beside him.

'OK, Lee. Where'd you get it?'

'Get what, Mr Parrish?' the young man slurred, waving a hand vaguely to disperse the smoke from his cigar.

'It's all over town that you're duded up in fancy store-bought duds and splashing money over the bar like it's water.'

'What's wrong with that?' Lee said, the words almost indecipherable as he tried to concentrate on the two difficult tasks of speaking and focusing his eyes on the lawman at the same time.

'You're coming with me,' the lawman said, firmly hauling the young man to his feet. Realizing his charge would not even be able to walk unaided, he added, 'You're gonna sleep off this skunk of a katzenjammer in the hoosegow. Then, when you've a semblance of a brain again, you're gonna explain your sudden largesse.'

'Large . . . large . . . what?'

'Largesse — it's fancy talk for grubstake. Now come on.'

4

Jim Catfoot and Ted Faulkner were sitting on the boardwalk outside the Wright County telegraph office. There had been a dispute between two local spreads over land. Threats had been made and a few shots exchanged but no one had been hurt yet. Along with the local lawman and his deputy, the two Pinkerton men had visited both ranch-owners in turn and managed to talk sense into them, advising them to get lawyers to do the talking. The agency superintendent had been right; the job there had been a piece of cake: Agreements had been reached with no more gunplay, and the two agents had telegraphed the company's Western Division headquarters in Denver to report and seek further orders.

Eventually a message came back. It congratulated them on a successful completion but told them not to return yet and set them a new mission. They were the nearest officers in the field to a town called Ogden where a bank on the Pinkerton books had been robbed. They were to investigate.

* * *

Meanwhile in Ogden itself, Sheriff Joel Parrish faced a puzzle. There was a horse in the livery that looked very much like the one that had belonged to one of the recent bank robbers. Then Old Ma Roberts's lad had come into a couple of hundred dollars. That the young man had said that he had found them in a saddle-bag seemed to be confirmed when the sobered-up young man took him to the location of the find and revealed the discarded bags.

A couple of days on, the lawman's puzzle was solved when a corpse, and later a second, was brought in. Both had been found at the riverside downstream, water-sodden and each bearing a bullet hole. He'd called in the bank manager and some of the folk who had seen them around town together with the few who had been on the sidewalk at the time of the getaway. All confirmed that the corpses were those of the robbers.

One of the men had a screwed-up wanted poster in his pocket giving the name of Dick Bodeen. Trawling through his files, the sheriff had come up with a similar dodger on the man — and another that showed the second body to be that of a small-time no-good by the name of Billy Boy O'Hara.

★   ★   ★

Jim Catfoot and Ted Faulkner dropped from their horses outside the Ogden law office. They introduced themselves to the sheriff and showed their papers.

'I understand why you've come,' the lawman said, 'but it's all over. Sorted itself out. After the heist the two villains had a serious difference of opinion over

41

something, resulting in them throwing lead at each other — and the bulk of the loot got washed down the Arkansas.'

'Anybody see all this?' Catfoot asked.

'No, but I've been able to piece it all together.' The lawman gave a summary of developments and what he had learned.

'Seems to fit together,' Faulkner said. 'Wouldn't you say, Jim?'

'Maybe so,' Catfoot said, 'but we still got to dot the i's and cross the t's.'

'Well, these are the bozos,' the sheriff said, laying the two wanted posters on his desk. 'Now what can I do to help you?'

'Give us all the details, how the robbery was conducted and such, and exactly what's transpired since.'

'What were they carrying?' Catfoot asked when the lawman had finished telling them all what he knew.

The sheriff opened a cupboard and took out two cardboard boxes. The name of Bodeen was scribbled on one,

O'Hara on the other.

Catfoot picked through the contents, noted a crumpled wanted poster bearing a likeness of Bodeen. 'Vain bastard,' he observed. 'Couldn't resist toting his own dodger around, even though it could have identified him if he'd been pulled up by the law on some minor matter.'

They examined the other contents of the dead men's pockets: coins and a few bills, bits and pieces.

There was a photograph of a woman. It was creased and the bottom corner was frayed but there was enough left of the ornate lettering for one to make out the words 'Lock's Photographic Parlour'. He read out the name. 'That mean anything?'

It had no significance for the lawman.

'The missing bit — where part of it has come away — looks like a word beginning with D. Following the word 'Parlour' as it does, points to it being the name of the town.' He looked at his friend. 'Nearest big place within a hundred miles beginning with D is Denver, ain't it?'

'Yeah, give or take a hundred yards.'

'You know of a Lock's Photographic Parlour there?'

'No.'

'Neither do I,' Catfoot said, 'and I know every nook and cranny in Denver.' He pondered for a moment, then asked about the bodies.

'I delayed the burial when I heard Pinkerton was sending some guys. Got 'em stashed over at the town undertaker's.'

'Lead the way if you will, Sheriff.'

Outside the funeral parlour, the sheriff rested against a stanchion and started building a smoke. 'If you want me, I'll be here. I've seen all I want to of those two critters — on top of which they're beginning to stink to high heaven.'

In the darkness of a backroom of the funeral parlour, the agents surveyed the bodies. The sheriff had been right about

44

the smell. Catfoot opened out the wanted posters. 'Bring a lamp over,' he said to the undertaker.

'That's them all right,' he said after making a comparison between the pallid faces and the printed images. 'You agree, Ted?'

'Yeah. No doubt.'

Catfoot folded up the posters and tucked them away, then began to go through Bodeen's pockets. 'You check his sidekick's effects.'

'You won't find anything,' the undertaker said. 'Sheriff went through them, cleared out their trappings. Everything he found he's got over in his office.'

'Yeah, I know,' Catfoot said. 'We've seen the stuff, but won't do no harm to make our own check while we're here.'

After a minute's search, Faulkner stepped back. 'Yeah, nothing here.'

Suddenly Catfoot's fingers located something right at the bottom of Bodeen's vest pocket. He extracted an elongated white object. It was so thin and unobtrusive, sodden as a result of its time in the water, that it had obviously been mistaken by the sheriff for part of the material along the lumpy joint of the pocket bottom.

He carefully unravelled it and flattened it on a nearby bench. The writing was smudged but could be made out.

'Well, what do you know — a bill of sale. Huh, Bodeen had enough sense to carry some proof that his mount was his. Figure, in his line of work he didn't want to get picked up on a chickenfeed rap like hoss-stealing.' He pointed to the inscription. 'Double G brand. You know the outfit?'

The undertaker shook his head.

Catfoot carefully eased the chit into his own pocket and nodded in the direction of the corpses. 'OK, we've seen all we want to see. You can box 'em up for good now.'

Once more in the fresh air, he showed the crumpled piece of paper he had found on the body to the lawman. 'Bodeen was carrying a bill of sale for his mount,' he said, handing it to the sheriff.

'Jeez, how did I miss that?'

'Understandable. It was screwed up and tucked in at the bottom of a pocket. Seems he bought the hoss from some outfit called the Double G. Ever heard of it?'

The sheriff examined the smoothed out document and shook his head. The name had no significance for him either.

* * *

The two Pinkerton men stood at the river's edge. Ted Faulkner gazed into the distance, noting how the river meandered to the horizon. 'The loot will be spread over a hell of a distance by now. I guess there's maybe a thousand folk or more between here and the coast who've had a lucky day and already picked up a dollar here and a dollar there. That money's disappeared like snow in a heat wave. Ain't no chance of accounting for it. Figure nothing for us now but to get our hides back to Denver.'

They mounted up and returned along the trail.

Eventually Catfoot slowed his horse. The idea of returning to Denver and the empty apartment was nettling him. He could do with a reason not to go back for a while. But what? Then he hit on one.

'You go back to Denver,' he said. 'Put in a report on what we've learned and tell 'em I'm still working on the case.'

Faulkner looked across at his comrade and grimaced. 'What's the point? The case is closed. You're never gonna get the loot back.'

'Yeah, I know. But something's bugging me. I don't have to tell you what reputation the organization's got amongst the nation's villainry. Once it's known a trader's got a Pinkerton contract, his business never gets touched. Ever since the Adams Express deal the crooks have learned the Pinks never give up and will be after 'em till the day they're nailed.'

'True. But I can't see what that's got to do with this matter.'

'It's bugging me *why* Bodeen pulled the job. I ain't gonna feel right in my mind until I know the why. He was an experienced law-breaker. Must have known his trade, too, 'cos as far I know he'd never been caught. Leastwise, he'd never been held long enough for the law to get him into a court. He knew our reputation — that's why he left the Adams Express box in the railroad heist up in Oregon a while back. He knew better. So why does he chance taking on the Pinks this time? Hell, only a blind man wouldn't see the Pinkerton sign on the front of that bank. So why does he do it? Either because he was stupid, or because he was over-confident. I want to know which. If I dig through his record and find he's been stupid before, that could satisfy me, and I'll report back for regular duty.'

'Still can't see the point, Jim.'

'Call it a whim.'

'How long's this whim gonna take before it fizzles out?'

'Can't say. Couple of weeks or more.'

'They ain't gonna like that back at headquarters. Listen, Jim, I've gotta tell 'em the truth about the case, what's happened and that, as the agents in the field, our recommendation is that the file be closed.'

Catfoot thought about it. 'Tell 'em I'm hanging back a spell sorting out loose ends.'

'There ain't no loose ends, Jim.' He paused, then added reflectively. 'I've heard it said that once an idea lodges in a Texan's head, hell and high water can't uproot it. Never knew the truth of it until I met you.'

His colleague swung a playful fist at him. 'How many times do I have to tell you, city boy, that I'm Californian not Texan. I know that's difficult for an Easterner to understand, but there's a difference.'

'Well, if there is a difference, my fine-feathered Californian friend, then I don't know it. See, I'm just a no-account Eastern city boy.' He waggled his head as he said the last bit.

Catfoot chuckled, then became serious. 'I'll come clean, Ted. There's another reason why. Fact is, I'd appreciate having a break from Denver for a spell. The place holds too many bad memories at the moment.'

'How come?'

'Couple of days before I joined you on the Wright County job, the missus left — ran off with some feller.'

'Hell, Jim, you didn't say.'

'No, I didn't. You're a good pal, and I should have said something, but it ain't a thing a guy's proud of.'

Faulkner pondered on the news. 'Flo's leaving — think it's a flash in the pan, something she'll get over?'

'No, the more I think back, the more I can see our marriage has been a bum steer for quite a spell. And, the time I'm on the road, away from home, she had plenty of time to find a more suitable feller. Had to happen some time, I figure. But it still came as a blow. And leaves a nasty taste in the mouth.'

'Gee, I'm sorry, Jim.'

'Thanks. So truth is, Denver's got bad memories for me just at the moment — and will have until I've adjusted.'

Faulkner thought about it. 'OK, if your mind's plain set on this then I'll tell the office you've stayed back so you can go downstream to see if you can find any trace of the money. I'll have to tell them that we think the possibility's remote but have agreed a little effort should be put into it, just to make sure we can't recover any. I think they'll buy that.'

'If there's any argument, tell the super I'm taking that week he said I was due. That should cover it.'

'OK, but even so, you're gonna have some explaining to do if you're much longer. The agency ain't gonna be happy paying your wages simply for you to follow a whim with not much expectation of a return to the company.'

'I'll take my chances. Anything to stay out of Denver for a spell.' He looked up at the darkening sky. 'Now we'd better get back to town before the heavens open.'

★ ★ ★

They'd gone to sleep with the patter of rain against the window and the sound of distant thunder and lightning, and next morning, Catfoot woke to the drip, drip, drip on the windowsill. He rose and threw a glance at his snoring comrade. Hauling on his clothes, he went to the window and looked down at the street. It had been a thunderous night but at least the rain had now stopped.

After breakfast they went outside where the earth of the street was soft underfoot after the downpour. In the stable Catfoot checked his horse while his colleague prepared his own mount for the return journey.

'You still sure about this little diversion of yours?' Faulkner said when he was finally mounted.

'Yeah.'

'Well, hope you turn up something. And sorry about you-know-what. See you, Jim.'

Catfoot watched his friend ride out of town then he headed along the boardwalk. His first step was to find out whatever was on file on Bodeen. That meant sending telegraph wires to headquarters and various law agencies.

'Sorry, mister,' the operator said when he enquired at the telegraph office. 'Wire's down. Must have been a lightning strike on the cable during the storm. Or maybe a telegraph pole's down some place.'

'How long will it take before I can get a message out?'

'Depends how long it takes to find the fault, then there's time to fix it. I figure at least a couple of days.'

Catfoot breathed a 'shoot' on being

stymied. Then: 'Where's the nearest telegraph office from here?'

'That'll be Latchford.'

'And how far's that?'

The man grimaced while he estimated the distance. 'A good hour's ride west of here.' Then added, 'But I don't recommend you putting in any time on the journey. There's more than an even chance they're affected by the same break in the line — in which case their system will be down too.'

'Thanks.'

Outside he thought about it, then decided to take the chance. A few hours on horseback would be time better spent than lazing around town with nothing to do but get plumb irritated.

5

The operator in Ogden had guessed right: the line in Latchford was dead too, as Catfoot found. In order that the journey would not be a complete waste, he called at the law office. The sheriff there rubbed his bristled chin as Catfoot explained the situation and made his inquiries. 'Can't help you, mister. Latchford is a quiet town. We don't get things like bank robberies. Nothing exciting at all.'

He opened his drawer and pulled out a bottle. 'Shot of rye?'

'No, thanks. Still too early in the day for me.'

'Not even for medicinal purposes?'

'You've talked me into it.'

'Fact is,' the sheriff continued after he'd hit the back of his throat with a slug, 'only exciting thing that's happened here in recent times is somebody heard gunfire the other day.' He chuckled and added, 'That's the height of news in this place.'

'Gunfire?' Catfoot said quizzically, putting down his empty glass. 'When?'

The sheriff couldn't be sure of the exact date but it could have been around the time of the robbery.

'And what was it all about?' Catfoot asked.

'Farmer came to town to get supplies. Said he heard a handful of shots along the trail on the way in. That's nothing, of course. Could have been somebody hunting. Sure ain't nothing to get hot under the collar about, but the old feller thought it might be more than that because he'd seen some riders out that way. I still wasn't interested — they could still have been hunters — but he kept on. Anyways, I had business out in those parts later in the day so I stopped by to investigate — just so I could shut up the old sodbuster next time he dropped in the office — but as I expected I found nothing out of kilter.'

'This farmer, what did he tell you about these fellers?'

The sheriff shook his head. 'To tell the truth I can't remember. Old Man Gibson, he's a bit of chatterbox, and I confess I paid little heed while he blathered on.'

'How far out is his place?'

'You going back to Ogden?'

'Reckon so.'

'Well, if you want to talk to him it's on your way.'

He explained the location of the Gibson place. Catfoot thanked him and returned to his horse.

★ ★ ★

The Gibsons had a fenced-off quarter section a distance off the trail.

'First thing I saw was these two riders,' the old man said in response to Catfoot's questions. 'Riding at a hell of a clip.'

'Which direction were they coming from?'

'From the river.'

'That means they could have been coming from Ogden.'

'Could be, but don't know. See, they were riding north so if they'd come from Ogden and crossed the river, they wouldn't have used the ferry. Not from the angle they were riding. If they had come from Ogden, they couldn't have known the area, otherwise they'd have used the ferry. The river being up the way it is since the rains, it would have been a hell of a mother to ford.'

'Yeah, I used the ferry myself on the way in.' Catfoot thought about it, then said, 'On the other hand, maybe they did know of the ferry but had a reason for not using it — like they didn't want to be seen.'

'Why would that be?'

'Well, there'd been a bank robbery in Ogden around that time and I'm investigating it. That's why I'm here.'

'Well, I'll be — '

'Go on with your tale.'

'Well, then a third rider comes out of the trees and heads towards them. Gave all the appearance he was expecting them.'

'What did they look like?'

'Can't say. Too far off to make out details. Anyways, last thing I saw they joined up. I thought nothing of it until a little while later I heard gunfire. Of course, in open country it's difficult to say where sound comes from but I'd say it was behind me. That is, from the direction where I'd seen these fellers.'

'What did you do?'

'I cracked the ribbons to get the hell out of there! Told the sheriff about it when I got to town but he wasn't really interested.'

'Huh,' his wife added from the background. 'Only thing that man's interested in is what's inside a bottle.'

Catfoot thought about it. 'This guy who joined them, did he have spare horses or something?'

'Nope, just a lone rider. Didn't break

from the trees until they showed up. Seemed to me he'd been keeping under cover.'

'Mebbe he was just waiting in the shade.'

'Who knows what's in a man's mind?'

'Anything else you can tell me?'

The old man puckered his grizzled eyebrows, then shook his head saying, 'No, that's about the size of it, younker.'

Catfoot accepted their offer of a cup of coffee, feigned polite interest in the oldster's chatter for a short while, then took his leave.

Back in the saddle he mulled the matter over. So if this was the bank gang, there were *three* of them. But why three? In a heist, the only role he could think of for another man standing by out of town would be tending fresh horses to give the gang an edge should a posse be after them. But the oldster had said there were no extra horses. So why would the third man be there? Didn't seem logical. You sure don't want to split three ways with a guy who has no active role in the heist.

Mebbe he was the brains. But Catfoot discounted that. On the limited information he had, Bodeen was the brains behind his own heists and hadn't shown any need for someone else to organize things. Mebbe the original intention had been for the fellow to participate in the robbery but he had suffered some injury on the journey and at the last minute was not deemed capable of direct participation.

Or mebbe these three fellers were nothing to do with the bank job at all.

★   ★   ★

He headed back late afternoon. For no other reason than it seemed to be the natural base for his operations, and knowing of no other large town in the area, he'd decided to return to Ogden. But before leaving the Gibson place he'd asked if there were any settlements on his way back where he could visit and ask questions. The old man had suggested if he arced north a mite he could take in Baggs on the return journey. 'But might not be worth the trouble,' Gibson had added, explaining that it was nothing more than a shack that served as saloon-cum-general store run by Nathan Baggs, from whom the place got its name.

The old man was right. Just a wooden sprawl made up of tacked-on afterthoughts away from the trail in the middle of a flat nowhere. Catfoot watered his horse at the trough outside, then went in to buy a drink and ask his questions. Nathan Baggs, a big bluff fellow with the vestiges of an English accent, looked at Catfoot's pieces of paper but neither he or his single other customer could offer anything useful. Finally, Catfoot pulled the bill of sale from his pocket and handed it across the bar. 'You know this horse brand?'

The man shook his head. 'I'm afraid I have not seen it before, sir. Off trail like this, we get few passing strangers in here. Serving locals is our main purpose.'

After showing it to the other drinker with equal lack of success, Catfoot returned it to his pocket. 'Any horse traders hereabouts? They might recognize it.'

'No,' Baggs said. 'Something like that is too fancy a business for these parts. Folks around here are farmers doing all they can to scratch a simple living out of the soil.'

'Nathan's right,' the other said. 'Fact is, nearest horse outfit is Jeff Nolan's.'

'That far?'

'Couple of hour's ride, wouldn't you say, Nathan?'

'Mebbe more.'

'Which direction?'

'Kinda north.'

'This Jeff Nolan — he know the horse business throughout the territory?'

'And beyond.'

With no tight leads, investing time in visiting Nolan would be better than nothing. It was just a matter of deciding whether to postpone the visit till the next day.

'Going to Nolan's — would it be better to start from Ogden or here?'

Baggs had no difficulty in the calculation. 'Starting from here would give you an edge of some fifteen miles.'

That would mean staying the night at the Englishman's place. 'You got a pallet and food?'

'Both. How does salt pork and beans sound? With a choice of American coffee or English tea.'

★ ★ ★

The sun was marking noon the next day when he finally made the horse ranch. Nolan was an accommodating man. 'Yeah,' he said when shown the bill of sale. 'The Double G. That's George Granger's mark. Know him well.'

'Where's his place?'

'Some ways east of here.'

'You got a map?'

'Yeah, some place.'

When he eventually located the thing, he unrolled it across his desk. He donned eyeglasses and peered at the document, his index finger working a trail across the cracked surface. Then: 'There. Out near Sunny Ridge.'

Catfoot examined the area, eventually murmuring, 'I wonder.' He could see that the nearest place of any size to the Granger spread was Dodge City.

'Yeah, I wonder,' he mouthed again. Dodge City was the kind of place that would boast a photographic parlour. And it began with a D. Of course. Why had he not thought of Dodge?

He thanked the man and took his leave. Still with nothing else to go on, he decided to pursue the faint clue. With all his effects on his horse's back, there was no need to return to Ogden. He would go straight to Dodge.

6

Once he hit the Arkansas, the trail was a clear one, his task just a matter of following its muddy ribbon all the way to Dodge. That was the good news. The bad news was his queries continued to draw blanks at every town and settlement along the route.

It was long lonely ride too, allowing him to brood over his wife's leaving. She was a damn fine woman. Why had he let it happen? Again the notion of complacency came to the fore. Life was all about learning lessons, and he'd learned a new one: don't take your woman for granted.

But his brooding went onto the back burner when he hit a town that had a working telegraph link with Denver and he wired the office to see if they had any information on Bodeen.

At headquarters they kept files on

criminals and outlaws. The idea of keeping such records — rather than just treating each case as a brand new one — was relatively new; an idea that the founder of the agency had borrowed from England's Scotland Yard. The police across the water had recently started doing it — along with applying scientific methods to their work — and were finding the procedure of considerable help in tackling London's criminal fraternity.

Forever seeking to make his operation efficient, Alan Pinkerton had initiated the system of record-keeping in his own business.

Denver came back but said the search would take some time as they would have to contact Chicago and New York. He checked with the telegraph operator who told him most of the towns along his route had a wire office. All he had to do was check with them whenever he had the opportunity. So he pressed on.

He knew that the clippings and

documents on some criminals filled a cardboard box while the records of others amounted to no more than a few lines on a piece of paper. It was a paradox that the volume of information the agency had did not reflect the importance of a lawbreaker. By the nature of things, the most successful criminals would be adept at keeping their nose below the parapet. Origins were unknown, little would be known of their associates, while physical descriptions were hazy or non-existent.

He was bunking in a small town on the Arkansas when the Denver office finally came back on his request — and he was to learn that Bodeen was such a character. The message consisted of a mere couple of lines. While not quite top of the agency's wanted list, Bodeen was way up but, as a consequence of successfully keeping out of the lime-light, there were no bulging folders in his dossier. Apart from the Oregon railroad knock-over there was a list of jobs in which he was only a suspect.

In his rented room, Catfoot mused on the message from his employer. At least it didn't ask what the hell he was playing at, or order him to get his ass back to head-quarters. That was a plus. But the missive threw up a conundrum. It was recorded how Bodeen had given himself away on the Oregon job. The detective pondered on it. Why would such a high-ranking criminal — with little known officially about him — why should he deliberately divulge his identity as Bodeen had done during the Oregon railroad heist?

After a meal, he checked in at the law office and presented his credentials to the sheriff ensconced in a swivel chair behind a desk.

'You know this guy?' Catfoot asked, handing over Bodeen's poster.

The man's first response was to rub his nose reflectively as his eyes flicked over the image. Then: 'No, but I figure I got the same dodger somewheres. You after him?'

'No. The guy was shot dead after a

70

heist over in Ogden. I'm trying to check his backtrail, learn something about his previous doings, find something about his connections. I'm keen to find out who he knew and who he might have worked with.'

'Well, he didn't come from these parts.'

'You didn't see him or someone like him riding through? He'd have a sidekick, mebbe two.' He showed the dodger bearing Billy Boy O'Hara's features. 'This was one of them but I haven't got anything on the third.'

The sheriff shook his head again. 'Sorry, pal, can't oblige.'

Catfoot's spirits remained low. Even in bleak, sparsely populated country like the West, a man didn't travel without leaving some kind of mark. Catfoot was fast coming to the conclusion that Bodeen was a new-comer to working in the region.

Not for the first time the phrase 'wild goose chase' came to his mind. But the notion was soon to be given an eviction notice. As his usual last shot, he showed the picture of the girl from Bodeen's pocket. 'Know her?'

'No.'

Catfoot was about to return the photograph to his pocket when the sheriff added, 'Don't know the gal but funny thing is, had this mug of mine subjected to photographic chromatism in the self-same establishment.'

'You did? Where?'

The lawman proudly indicated the shield on his chest and jerked a thumb at the wall to which was pinned a portrait of him brandishing his six-gun in a theatrical pose. 'Had it took not long after I donned the badge. You know, to commemorate my appointment. Good likeness, eh?'

'Yeah,' Catfoot said absently. His mind was more occupied with the legend inscribed beneath the picture of the posturing lawman. In ornate lettering ran the words, 'Lock's Photographic Parlour — Dodge City'.

'I was right,' he said.

The sheriff looked puzzled. 'How's that?'

Catfoot showed his photograph again. 'See the D, where the picture's been ripped? I was guessing — and hoping — that the word spelled Dodge. Now I'm sure.'

'Yeah. Lock's Photographic Parlour, Dodge City.'

'Whereabouts in the town is it?'

'Can't miss it. Close to the stockyards.'

Catfoot gave his thanks and returned to his lodgings, eager for an early night — and an early start next morning.

★   ★   ★

He left before most of the town was up and the light was still grey over the Arkansas. For the first time he had a connection. There was every chance that Bodeen had been through Dodge. If so, maybe Catfoot could pick up a few more details there and hopefully something on the third rider. Then, if he got called back to head-quarters, at least he would have filled in a little more about the outlaw's background and maybe his mysterious associate. That way he could return to regular duties, knowing that his quest had not been entirely in vain.

He was thinking on this when the horse juddered and came to a standstill, nickering plaintively. He dropped down and immediately saw there was a problem with a leg. He cursed to himself. Such had been his single-mindedness in his inquiries that he had failed to take account that he might be exhausting the animal. Unforgivably for him he'd paid no heed to the possibility of over-working the creature.

He checked. The horse could walk slowly but not take weight.

Luckily he wasn't far from his destination, but it was dark by the time he saw the lights of Dodge City in the distance.

7

As the railhead of the Santa Fe, Dodge City was the latest of the cowboy capitals where the cattle businesses bringing their herds up from Texas could find a market. In their turn, towns like Wichita, Newton and Hays City had enjoyed a boom as they had briefly become the most westerly end-of-track point. Then, as the railroad progressed, the thing would quiet down.

But now it was Dodge's turn, as witnessed by the bustle and noise that greeted Catfoot as he walked his horse along the main drag. The constant lowing of the animals in their pens droned through the night air as Catfoot worked his way through the town. In the distance across the tracks he caught the glow of what he guessed was the famed house of ill-repute known as the Red Light House — so called because of the light shining through the red glass of its frontage which acted as a night beacon to carousing cowboys as they emptied out of saloons.

Starved of a woman's touch, he mused for a moment on joining the noisy revellers as they staggered across the tracks. But he was tired, and he reminded himself he had more important things to do before he paid heed to such needs.

He found a livery stable to quarter his horse, then a place to rest his own head: a drover's shack beside a stinking mountain of buffalo hides.

★ ★ ★

After breakfast next morning he stepped out onto Front Street. Like any westerner, he knew about Dodge, even though he'd never been to it: Hell Street, Boot Hill, the Red Light District with its infamous name now being quickly applied to houses of ill-repute in other towns.

With the benefit of daylight, the

pattern of the town's brief history as a railhead could be seen in its layout. Near the railroad were the substantial buildings. Then, north and south, the sprawl of shacks, lean-tos and varied ramshackle structures. A vast array of tents housed the rest of the population from freighters to bullwhackers.

Strolling past noisy drovers and buffalo-hunters with their hide-laden wagons, he made his way along the main drag, until he got to the livery.

'Had a chance to look your horse over,' the man said. 'Nothing bad by my reckoning so don't think we need to call the horse doctor over. Signs are a bad sprain, is all. Needs rest and watching to see how it develops.'

'What kind of delay are we talking of?'

'Your guess is as good as mine, pilgrim. A week, say.'

Catfoot thought on it, then slipped the man some bills. 'That should cover looking after him for a few days. I'll be back when I've sorted out my plans.'

His next stop: Lock's Photographic Parlour. The proprietor was in the backyard where he was taking advantage of the strong sunlight to capture his images. Against a painted backdrop of an ornamented garden stood a suited young man, his one hand pompously holding a derby hat at an angle, his other hand resting proudly on the shoulder of a girl. The heads of man and woman were clamped by vices from behind.

'Won't be long, sir,' the technician said as he saw the visitor enter the enclosure.

Catfoot watched as the man flitted around his subjects, primping here, smoothing there. Then the man returned to his contraption where he removed the lens and counted to ten. After a repetition of the procedure, Catfoot could see the session was coming to an end and took the photograph from his pocket. 'I'm interested in this picture.'

'Ah, yes, sir. I remember it well. One of my best studies.'

'You remember it well enough to recall the girl's name?'

'Of course. The personage is no less than Gypsy Jane herself, one of our local celebrities.'

'And where can I find this Gypsy Jane?'

'Star feature at the Eldorado.'

★ ★ ★

On the other side of town away from the cattle pens, the Eldorado was the most impressive building on Main Street, its false front thrusting into the pewter sky. Emanating from the batwings over the monkeyhouse din he could hear singing, to the accompaniment of a jangling piano.

He crossed the street and, unnoticed by the occupants, paused inside the entrance to get his bearings. The source of the voice was a woman at the far end on a stage consisting of boards laid across beer kegs. The air was a thin soup, its odour a mishmash of cigarettes and beer.

He strolled over to the bar that covered the length of the room. He lit a cigarette, ordered a beer and took it standing, while keeping his eye on the singer. It was the girl in the photograph all right, but even at a distance he could see that the picture must have been taken a long time ago.

Two cigarettes later, the songbird finished her warbling and, against a background of half-hearted clapping, she went to the bar.

He joined her. 'Buy you drink, ma'am?'

She gave him the once-over. 'Yeah. But no strings.'

He chuckled as he waved a hand to catch the bartender's attention. 'No strings.'

From a distance the woman had some feminine allure but proximity told a different story. The gaudy lipstick had been smeared on without precision and thick powder clung to her face.

After the shot glasses had been placed before him, he gestured to a vacant table. 'Like to sit down a spell, miss?'

'What for?'

'To talk.'

'I said no strings. Thanks for the drink, mister, but we got nothing to talk about.'

He took a swig of his drink and said, 'Would it make any difference if I mentioned the name Bodeen?'

There was a visible reaction in her features that she tried to mask.

He left it for moment, then said, 'You didn't answer my question.'

'You law?'

'No.' A long ways back Catfoot had settled his conscience with the notion that there was a difference between lying and half-truth.

'Then what's your interest in him? What's your connection?'

'Let's say we — he and I — are in the same line of business.' Another half-truth that satisfied the circumstances.

She gave him a hard look-over, then said, 'OK, get me another drink — a large one — and we'll talk awhile.'

A minute later they were sitting with fresh glasses alongside a table at which a foursome of drovers were shooting craps.

'You mentioned Bodeen,' she said. 'Where is he? How is he?'

'So you know him. When was the last time you saw him?'

'For somebody who claims not to be a lawman you sure ask questions like one.'

'I've told you I'm not. So when was the last time you saw him?'

'A few months back. Said he had some business, then vamoosed.'

'What kind of business?'

'Don't know. It involved travelling, I know that much. He was always pulling up his picket-pin. But he always came back.' She leaned forward. 'Will you answer me like a decent feller? I asked where is he, how is he?'

He ignored her questions and continued with his own. 'Were you close to him? He mean something to you?'

Her face registered something against one of his words. 'What do you mean *were?*'

He eyed her. 'You OK to take some bad news?'

'Like what?'

'I'm afraid, ma'am, he's dead.'

She closed her eyes and swayed. Then: 'How, where?'

'Place called Ogden. He was killed after knocking over the bank there.'

She let out a long sigh then, eyes still closed, whispered, 'So *that* was the big deal he was talking about.'

Oblivious to their conversation, the players at the adjacent table continued their game until a roar indicated that the craps had fallen in a pattern that meant a big win for some lucky drover.

'So you *were* close to him,' Catfoot concluded.

She didn't speak so he added, 'And you knew something was in the offing.'

His words brought her out of her trance and she cleared her throat. 'So he's not coming back . . . there's no big

deal pulled off . . . and no great future.'
The words stumbled out almost inaudibly as though she was talking to herself.

'I'm afraid that's the size of it.'

She sniffed.

'I'm real sorry, ma'am, but that's the way the cards fall sometimes.'

'Huh, cards! Seems I could have done better staking my future *at* the card table. Not that I've got the money to throw at a card game, but at least that way I would have seen the circumstances in which my life went down the privy.'

In the glare of the overhead lamps her face had taken on a new bleakness, her features more crumpled, tear trails distorting the powder on her cheeks. 'Never trust a man. Mr Whatever-your-name-is.'

'That's a lesson I've learned too, ma'am, but not in the same circumstances.'

She breathed deeply in an effort to recompose herself. 'Yet another of life's slaps in the face that a creature has to get used to. Very well, I'll adjust to this one, too. I always do. Plenty of fish in the sea, they say.'

Alongside them on the wall was a mirror decorated with the etchings of a beer advertisement. She stretched her neck to look into it and observed the tearsmeared make-up. 'Jehosophat. I'm due back on stage in five minutes. If you'll excuse me, I have to attend to my face. I look a mess.'

She stood up and hurried, head down, across the floor to a door at the side of the bar. He waited five minutes and took another drink. Ten minutes passed and on the quarter hour he went to the bar. 'I thought the lady was singing again.'

The barman shook his head. 'Not today, mister. For some reason she's excused herself.'

'You mean she's gone?'

'I mean, if you're one of her many admirers, you're gonna be deprived of her singing today.'

'Where does she live?'

The man shook his head. 'Walk on by, mister. Rule of the house: we don't give out the girls' addresses.'

Catfoot circled the bar and pushed past the barman who had moved in an attempt to stand in his way. The Pinkerton man went through to the back with the barman hot on his tail shouting, 'Hey, mister.'

The place was empty.

'This is a private area, mister. Customers ain't allowed back here.'

'And you're not going to tell me where she lives?'

'Nope,' the barman said sharply. But after a second, his demeanour changed. He winked and added, 'But if it's a girl you want, I can give you some other addresses.'

With a, 'Not today, thanks,' Catfoot went out the back door and looked along the alley. But there was no one.

Over at the law office he gave his name and showed his papers. 'You know where the gal who sings at the Eldorado lives?'

'Gypsy Jane?' the lawman said. 'Last I heard she got rooms over at the Republic Rooming House. What's this all about?'

'Wish I could oblige, Sheriff, but I can't give details 'cos there just ain't no details to give. Following up a loose end on a case is all. She got a feller?'

The man laughed. 'Gypsy Jane! If you're looking for a particular feller you'll have to check out a whole queue of sweaty-palmed, lip-licking *hombres*.'

'Any of 'em prominent?'

'Listen, mister, she's a gal who offers services other than singing — for a fee. The town's Women's Committee grouses but, as long as there's no trouble, I don't intervene. And I certainly don't keep tabs on her clientele.'

'How do I get to this Republic?'

Outside he pondered on what he had learned. So Gypsy Jane knew lots of men. That increased the possibility of the notion that she had been in cahoots with the mystery man who had been waiting in the trees. This Mr X had been one of the threesome involved in the bank knockover at Ogden but it sure looked now like he had secretly planned a double-cross. Yet the woman's tears had seemed real enough when he had told her of Bodeen's death. An experienced detective, Catfoot reckoned he could tell when someone was faking such things. She did seem to have been genuinely shocked. That opened up the possibility that, while she had been close to Bodeen at some time, things had cooled between them, and that she knew of the mystery man's planned double-cross but it hadn't been part of the scheme that Bodeen should have been killed. It was that that would have caused the shock.

When he located the Republic he found it to be little more than a downtown flop joint.

'Gypsy Jane!' the lady owner exclaimed when he made inquiries. 'When you find the hussy, you let me know. Heard a commotion, saw her leaving. Went to her room, found it cleaned out. Couldn't see hide nor hair of her when I got out to the street. Hell, did she move quick! And the cat owes me two weeks' rent!'

'She leave alone?'

'Got some feller with her.'

'You know who?'

'No.'

'What did he look like?'

'Can't say. Just caught a glimpse of their backs as they went through the lobby door. And she with all her belongings wrapped up in a carpetbag. I was only partly dressed at the time and in the short spell it took me to make myself respectable, they'd disappeared.'

'Can I have a look at her room?'

Her demeanour softened. 'You thinking of renting it?'

'Afraid not, ma'am.'

She showed no sign of cooperation but when he identified himself she reluctantly gave him permission. But there was nothing. Just like the old gal had said, the place had been cleaned out with nothing to show of its former occupant.

He enquired at the livery stable but no horses had been taken. There was a possibility the pair had got their own horses.

Outside he looked at the darkening sky. Not only night, but also rain was coming. Using his own horse was out of the question and, by the time he would have bought a replacement, it would be completely dark. Not the best conditions for heading out into unknown terrain without much idea about which direction he should be taking.

He called in at a saloon and ruminated on his next step. Then it hit him. Why horses? They could be travelling by stage! He asked the whereabouts of the depot and made his way to the street, threading his way through the beginnings of the rain.

At the stage depot, he learned that a man and woman *had* bought tickets just before the conveyance had left.

'The woman,' he asked of the booking clerk, 'was she Gypsy Jane from the Eldorado?'

'I couldn't tell you, sir. The Eldorado is not a place I frequent. The missus would have my hide should I ever set foot in such a place.'

'Well, what did she look like?'

'Kinda exotic. You know, features painted like one of them Jezebels from the Red Light district.'

'And the man?'

'Big feller, wide-brimmed hat, one of them bulky foul-weather jackets — about all I can tell you.'

'Thanks. And where's the stage headed?'

'Low Water Creek.'

Catfoot looked out of the window. The rain was turning the main drag into a quagmire. Heading out that night on horseback was not an option. He went over to a map on the wall. Low Water Creek was fifty miles or more across open land. With his own animal not likely to be serviceable for the best part of a week he'd already reconciled himself to the fact he was going to have to part with it. And he reckoned that fifty miles of bleak country was too far and hazardous for him to ride on an untried horse, if he had the choice of other transport. 'When's the next stage out?'

'Not till tomorrow, sir.'

Catfoot muttered 'shoot' to himself and thanked the man. Outside he mulled over events. Everything pointed to the fellow in the foul-weather jacket being the Mr X from the Ogden job, the latest man-friend of Gypsy Jane. Things were fitting into place. A member of the gang, he had planned a double-cross. He had stayed back from the actual heist for some reason — the reason still puzzled the detective — maybe something unplanned had cropped up, like the fellow sustaining some injury on the journey to Ogden. But nothing to date indicated the man had any serious injury so possibly he had feigned it so that he wouldn't put himself at risk on the job. And, not exerting himself, the fellow would be that much fitter for pulling his double-cross. Then he could have kept the bulk of the take and used some of the money to fix it like the lot had been washed down the river. That would explain why, when the fellow had returned to Dodge, he hadn't scooted. With the authorities thinking only two had been involved in the caper and Bodeen and O'Hara dead, he'd have no reason to bolt.

Catfoot went to the telegraph office with the intention of wiring ahead to Low Water Creek requesting the law there to keep a surreptitious eye on the couple until he got there.

'Sorry, sir,' the operator said. 'There's no line out of Low Water yet. The company are planning one but they're not linked to the network yet. They're talking about laying a line next year.'

'Well, that's no good to me now,' Catfoot grunted. 'You linked to Denver?'

'Of course, sir.'

Better than nothing. At least he could keep headquarters informed. He dictated his message. 'Re: Odgen case. Figure might have been a double-cross. Am following a lead.'

He pushed payment across the counter, adding, 'And you tell no one of this message.'

'Indeed, sir. Confidentiality is company policy.'

He was back on the street when he heard his name called. He turned to see the telegraph operator trying to catch his attention. 'Message for you just come in from Denver, sir.'

Huh, he thought, at last the office was getting off its ass.

He scanned the paper. 'Bodeen known to have associated with John Logan. Also known as Big Jack Logan.'

Not much, but all the signs he had been getting was that the fellow he was after was of a bulky build — and the sobriquet 'Big Jack' squared with that description. Things were looking up.

With a nod of thanks he headed towards the depot to book passage on the next day's stage. Resuming his journey the following day would mean that he'd not be in pursuit as quickly as he would have liked, but at least he would appreciate the rest. And the delay was compensated by the fact that now he had a name.

8

The sun was high and still climbing when the stage rolled up the following morning to where Catfoot had been impatiently waiting on the Dodge boardwalk. A few puddles in the main drag were the only signs of the previous evening's rain.

He watched the driver haul on the handbrake and drop down. As the man unlatched the carriage door, Catfoot took the opportunity to ask him about the previous day's passengers.

'Sorry, pal, wasn't my run,' the driver said, as he gestured for folk to board.

Catfoot waited until the other passengers had entered. Then he stepped up into the vehicle and tipped his hat to an elderly lady and young girl, whom he guessed was her daughter, already seated. There was some foreign accent to the older woman's speech when she returned a clipped, 'How do you do?' He took a seat alongside them and pushed an elbow out of the window.

They heard the driver haul himself into position, there was a whip-crack and they were away. As soon as the vehicle left the flattened surface of the town's street and hit the rough trail, wheels crunched and the vehicle began a constant lurch this way and that.

Catfoot eyed the other occupants: directly opposite him a young rangy fellow in the garb of a drover; next to him a short fellow, the only occupant with no evidence of burning by the sun and sporting a neat derby and covert-cloth topcoat, had an appearance suggestive of some kind businessman; finally at the end, what looked like a wealthy cattleman, a deeply-bronzed guy in a ten-gallon hat with an ornate cow-horn tie clip.

There were brief exchanges between the strangers but when enough had been said to meet the requirements of politeness, there was quiet again, save for the creaking of the wooden frame and grind of steel rims against gravel.

Catfoot looked out of the window to observe the wild landscape gradually giving way to flat, treeless terrain dotted with patches of mesquite and barrel cacti. With the sameness only interspersed with the occasional stand of organ pipe, his concentration lapsed and eventually his eyes closed.

His reverie was broken by a voice.

'Name's Chauncey Goodman, at your service, sir.'

Catfoot opened his eyes.

It was the man in the derby leaning toward him. 'Western representative of the Connecticut Merchandising Company,' the fellow went on.

Catfoot's only reciprocation was a nod. The man was obviously a drummer and, having no interest in being regaled with the virtues of the Connecticut Merchandising Company and their products, the Pinkerton man slumped down further into his seat and pushed his hat over his eyes.

Getting no more response from Catfoot, the drummer struck up a conversation with the man on his left whom Catfoot had assumed was a cattleman but whom, it transpired, was a horse dealer.

'Yes, sir,' the man said proudly, 'that's my line: horses.'

'Hah, the horse,' the drummer observed. 'A noble beast.' Then he chuckled, adding, 'I only know two things about the horse, and one of them is very coarse.'

With garbage like that coming out of the man's mouth, Catfoot was even more glad he had declined conversing with him. The horse trader was clearly of the same opinion because the interchange petered out at that point. Undeterred, the drummer struck up conversation with the elderly lady, eliciting that the couple were returning after visiting relatives in Low Water.

'That is very interesting,' the drummer said when he commented on her accent and learned she was originally a settler from Germany. 'I myself am half Pilgrim stock and half Pennsylvanian Dutch.'

Who cares? Catfoot thought, and was grateful when the coach pulled into a relay station.

After the lathered horses were brought to a stand-still, the occupants debouched and stretched. The station man pointed to the lone adobe building. 'Help yourselves to coffee and food, folks,' he said and, along with the driver, he set about changing the horses.

When the station man had finished, he came into the building and poured coffee for himself and the driver. Catfoot took his mug over to the table where the two men were sitting. 'The through-stage yesterday: there was a couple, a woman and feller.'

'Yeah, I remember,' the station man said.

'The gal went by the name of Gypsy Jane,' Catfoot said. 'You catch the guy's name?'

'Had no talkifying with them.'

'What did the feller look like?'

'Hefty guy.'

'Height?'

'Tallish, mebbe reached six feet.'

'Clothes?'

'Tan flat hat as I recall. Big, hide jacket.'

'Distinguishing marks? Scars, for example?'

The man shook his head. 'Listen, pal. I fix fresh horses. Ain't got no reason to write down detailed descriptions of passengers passing through.'

'Of course,' Catfoot said. 'I understand. I was just wondering is all.'

When the two workmen left the table to make final preparations outside, the drummer brought over his coffee mug and sat beside Catfoot. 'Couldn't help overhearing,' he said in his insidious way. 'You seem mighty interested in this feller. What's the story?'

Catfoot didn't even look at him. The man was a pain. 'You ask a lot of questions, pardner', Catfoot replied, drained his own cup and walked towards the door.

'Huh,' the drummer grunted, waited until the man was out of earshot and added, 'And *you* ask a lot of questions too, my uppity friend.'

Shortly they had all re-boarded and the coach resumed its passage, lurching onwards, leaving its mark beneath billowing dust clouds.

★   ★   ★

The harness chains were still jingling when Catfoot dropped down onto the hard ground of Low Water Creek's main street and headed into the stage office.

'Two incoming passengers on yesterday's stage,' he said, 'man and a woman — you spot 'em when they arrived, see which way they went?'

'Sorry, mister. Once folks have disembarked, ain't no concern of mine.'

Outside, Catfoot looked the town over. Even in the gloom of approaching sundown he could tell it wasn't the biggest place he'd ever seen. If he hung around for a while, he reckoned, it shouldn't be too difficult to find the pair. They had no cause to hide away, but even if they did hole up in some hotel room, they'd have to show themselves eventually.

He checked into a boarding house and spent the early evening watching the comings and goings of guests. After he'd checked with the clerk that he'd seen them all, he took a meal and then casually toured the saloons — but with no result.

Next morning the place looked even smaller in daylight. He could lob a rock from one end to the other. He noted the remaining hotels and boarding houses, systematically checking each one — again no leads. Hell, the couple couldn't have just disappeared.

If they'd left they would have needed horses so he questioned the proprietor of the town's only livery stable if he'd loaned out a couple of saddle-horses. The negative response suggested to him one last possibility — that maybe the pair lived locally and, on arrival, had simply walked out of town.

He returned to the stage depot. 'Two days ago, the incoming stage — who was the driver?'

The clerk sucked his pencil. 'Two days ago?'

'Yeah. You remember, the one I asked about last night.'

The man ummed, then said, 'Why, that'd be Old Cal Nelson. Yeah, he was filling in for the regular driver who'd called off sick.'

'And where does this Cal Nelson live?'

★ ★ ★

Cal Nelson's place was a frame shack with a tarpaper roof at the end of the drag.

'Yeah, I remember them.' the old-timer said. 'Beefy guy and a real looker of a woman. But they never got to town. Asked me to pull in at a place we call Frobisher Crossing.'

They'd dropped off before the town! *That* explained his problem in tracing them.

'And where's that?' the detective asked.

'Five miles back.'

'If I go out there, how will I recognize it? How's it marked?'

'There's a little bridge over the creek there. Can't miss it, the only bridge on the last part of the run.'

Catfoot cast his mind back and remembered the stage wheels clattering over it during his own journey in. 'Yeah, I recall.' Then: 'When they'd disembarked, you see which direction they headed?'

'Last time I saw 'em, they were walking up the grade alongside the bluff on the west side of the trail.'

'Where would they be going?'

'Beats me, pal. Ain't nothing out there that I know of.'

★ ★ ★

The town stretched to a livery with a selection of horses for sale. Catfoot looked them over and a handsome palomino took his fancy.

'I'd warn you against that one,' the man said. 'His name's Buck and it's a fitting name.' He pointed to a spot in the centre of the animal's left thigh. 'Got a real sore spot there. Don't know what it is. I've had a look and there's no lump or anything obvious, so don't seem serious. But he gets agitated if it's touched. And he can buck like hell.'

The agent glanced at the other horses and back at the palomino. 'Gotta say, he's still my preference out of the bunch. No reason why my foot will get anywhere near his sore spot in regular riding. I'll bear it in mind, but I been around horses all my life and don't see any trouble.'

'If you're sure?'

Catfoot stroked the animal's muzzle. 'We're gonna get along fine, ain't we, Buck?'

9

After buying provisions, Catfoot set out along the trail and before long came to the bridge. He dismounted and ground-hitched the palomino near the creek so the animal could drink. Then he stepped up onto the bridge and looked to the west.

The stream came along the base of the bluff that the stage-driver had earlier described. And, as the old man had said, it didn't seem to be going anywhere. No trail to speak of.

He mounted up and wended his way along the edge of the creek in the westerly direction. He regularly looked down, his eyes raking the ground for sign. Despite the fact that he found none, his motivation was not unduly dampened. For a start, he was intrigued as to why the couple would drop from a stagecoach and undertake an arduous journey on foot into a nowhere land. Either they knew the area, or were trying to lose themselves. If the latter was the case, then they would have to have a reason, a reason that Catfoot would like to know.

He mused in this way until he saw something that took his mind off its ramblings. A speck in the distance, a single rider heading his way. The man's posture in the saddle suggested an old fellow. In itself that was not out of the ordinary. What grabbed his attention was the man hastily dismounting from his mule and heading into the brush. Like he'd spotted Catfoot and was making himself scarce.

Catfoot reined in. His horse could do with a break anyhow. He took the animal slightly to one side, so that it could still be partially seen from ahead and might suggest to anyone watching that Catfoot was merely taking a rest near his horse. He allowed the animal to graze while he slipped behind a tree and took up a discreet vigil on the area where he had seen the man. In time he caught the flash of sunlight on metal. The fellow had climbed the grade and was now viewing the scene with a rifle at the ready.

Catfoot gave a reassuring pat to his animal and began to make his own way up the slope. Slowly he worked his way round till he was above the figure. He could make out the old man lying across the rock, gripping a rifle. The man turned his head slightly, ejected a stream of tobacco-juice and returned to studying the vicinity of the distant grazing horse.

Quietly Catfoot drew his handgun and eased himself down until he was close.

'Drop the rifle,' he commanded, 'and turn round — slow.'

The fellow juddered, assessed the situation, then did as he was bid, revealing in the process an ancient, weathered face decorated with a dirty grey beard.

'Don't try anything,' Catfoot said, as

he approached the oldster. With the gun jammed in the man's stomach, he patted the pockets. No obvious extra weaponry.

'Take that out,' he said when he sensed some kind of bulge in the man's jacket pocket.

He stood back while the old man extracted a hefty, drawstring bag.

'Some piece of change you got there,' Catfoot said when the man undid the bag to reveal a billfold. 'Go on, put it back. I ain't no road agent.'

'Obliged, mister.'

'OK,' Catfoot went on. 'Why you figuring on burning some powder my way?'

'Don't mean no disputation, mister,' the man stuttered. 'Just wary is all.'

Catfoot stepped down and picked up the rifle. 'Is this the local way to greet strangers to these parts,' he said, hefting the weapon, 'poking hardware in their direction?'

'No, mister. Just keeping a weather-eye till you passed.' He patted his pocket. 'You seen the mazuma I'm carrying. Can't be too careful.'

Catfoot weighed up the situation, saw anxiety still cutting notches in the fellow's forehead. 'I believe you,' he said eventually. Then: 'For an oldster, you spotted me from hell of a distance.'

'Mister, I got some years under my belt but my eyesight's still top-notch. Can still fetch my supper out of a tree at a hundred yards.'

Catfoot sheathed his own gun and shucked the loads from the rifle. He was about to hand it back when the fellow turned and staggered towards a tree.

'Where are you going?' Catfoot snapped.

'You dizzied me up, mister, coming at back of me like that,' the man said, fumbling at the front of his pants. 'Age ain't been as kind to my bladder as it has to my eyesight. I'm pissing myself here.'

'OK,' Catfoot said. 'But just make

sure your pecker is the only thing you pull out.'

The oldster leant steeply forward and thumped one hand against the tree. He groaned in relief as a noisy cascade hit the bark.

When the man had finished and fixed his buttons, Catfoot handed him his rifle, along with the shucked shells.

'I figure you're on the square too, young 'un,' the old man said as he looked at the rifle. 'You didn't take my grubstake and, if you was figuring on dropping me, you'd have done it afore now, so I'll come clean. Fact is I've only just come by the money and was a-feared you might be aiming to dry-gulch me.'

Catfoot smiled. 'OK. Let's mooch down together. Then you go your way, I'll go mine like nothing has happened.'

As they worked their way down through the trees, Catfoot could tell by the increasingly incessant chatter that the fellow was starved of talk.

'I live a few miles further up,' he said.

'On my ownsome. I'm particular about my company. Ain't found a living creature yet — man or woman — that I can abide under the same roof for more than a night or two. Anyways, every now and again I need a change so I'm heading to town to treat myself. My place will be empty while I'm away. You're welcome to use it if you're heading that way. Place ain't locked. Help yourself to buttermilk and biscuits if you've a mind.'

'Thanks. That's mighty friendly.'

'Anyways, I might as well tell you the whole story,' the old man said as they neared the bottom. 'This guy comes by yesterday, out of the blue. Offers to buy a horse and mule. Hell, they're both flea-bitten critters but he was willing to give me top dollar. Huh, offered double their value. Scads — enough for me to replace 'em *and* buy myself a good time to boot. That's where I'm heading now. Low Water Creek — you know it?'

'Yeah. I passed through a ways back.'

They reached the man's mule and

the oldster squinted into the sun. 'I should make town before sundown. Then, liquor, a woman. Hell, maybe even drop my hide in a tub of hot water.'

'I'll walk you on to my horse,' Catfoot said.

'This feller,' he continued, after the man had mounted and they were walking along the valley bottom. 'He must have been toting some trappings to want to buy both your mounts.'

'He had some trappings all right — in the shape of a gal. Mite purty too.'

That nugget told Catfoot he was on the right trail and a list of questions lurched into his mind: but he saw problems. Having received what he saw as a favour from the big fellow, the old man might feel a little protective towards him; could be suspicious of Catfoot and might not be willing to impart information. Catfoot had to be careful so he put some thought into phrasing his questions, posing them as nonchalantly as he could muster.

'I might have crossed trails with the happy couple a few days back. He was a big hunky guy. Now, this fellow you had dealings with, what did he look like? May be the self-same guy.'

'Yeah. Biggish, like you say.'

Catfoot restrained himself from pressing for a more detailed description, much as he wanted it. So he restricted himself to one more question, again posed in a casual manner. 'The happy couple, they say where they were headed?'

The other scratched at his beard, brown with the stains of tobacco drippings. 'That's the funny thing. They didn't seem to know where they were. Asked a lot of questions about the locality, towns and things.'

Reaching the palomino, Catfoot heaved himself into the saddle. 'Well, have a good time tonight, my friend. Paint the town red.'

The old man waved a hand. 'And don't forget — buttermilk, biscuits, whatever you find.'

Catfoot felt some satisfaction as he

turned into the slight breeze and resumed his journey. From what he had learned, the couple had all the characteristics of being on the run. Whatever their story he wanted to know it. And a little extra information: he had found out that they were as unfamiliar with the terrain as he was.

10

A day later, a long way on from the old man's cabin where he'd spent the night, Catfoot found himself mounting a grade and looking down into yet another valley. The breeze coming across the ridge was cool against his face and he reined in near a tree. Weary, he sat awhile letting his eyes take in the scene below, noting nothing but rocky terrain and tree-covered slopes. A bleak nowhere place. No sign of trails. He was considering which direction to take when his bladder suddenly reminded him it needed attention. He dropped out of the saddle, undid his pants buttons and relieved himself against a tree.

'The other guy did that, too.'

Startled by the sound of another human, he whirled round to identify the source of the comment. A young girl was standing on the grass to his side a little distance down the slope. How had he missed her? Then he noted she was not too far away from a large rock and he reckoned she must have been behind that.

'Did what?' he asked.

'Piss against that self-same tree.'

'Sorry, miss,' he said, turning his back on her as he fixed his buttons. 'If I'd have known you was there . . .'

'Don't pay it no never-mind, mister. I seen fellows pissing before.'

'Which other guy was this?'

The girl looked away. 'Queenie says I shouldn't talk to strangers.'

He chuckled humourlessly. 'As I recall, missy,' he said in a raised voice, 'it was you who started this here conversation by commenting on my micturating.'

'Don't know what mic — what that word means.'

'Don't worry about it. Who's Queenie?'

She ignored him so he left it for a while then tried another question.

'Which other guy were you talking of, the one that was emptying himself against the tree?'

'The one that came by this morning.'

'So somebody was here earlier. Was he alone?'

'No. Got a gal with him. She took a piss too.' She giggled. 'Squatted down over there.'

'What kind of horses they riding?'

'Fellow was on a hack that looked ready to fall down and the gal was on a stumpy mule.'

He raised a hand and chopped the air directly ahead of him. 'They pass on through?'

'No, they paid our place a visit.'

'Your place?' he prompted, as he made a quick three hundred and sixty degree scan and saw nothing. 'Where's that?'

'Yonder.' She pointed to the right slope. 'In the trees. Can't see it from here. Fact, can't rightly see it from anywheres. Figure that's why we don't get many visitors.'

'Your place, what is it, a town?'

'S'pose you'd call it that.'

'It got a name?'

'We just call it the Place.'

He rubbed his aching limbs and checked the rapidly falling sun. 'This Place, it got somewhere that a guy can get a bed for the night and maybe some breakfast in the morning?'

'Figure so. Come on, mister.'

He took the reins of his horse and led it down the slope. As he descended he noted that there were still no perceptible trails in sight. The girl skipped along but kept her distance from him.

He followed her to the bottom. Part way along the valley floor she turned right between rocks and worked her way up through trees. It was a tortuous, unmarked route and he understood why they didn't get many visitors.

'How far to go?' he asked when he still could see no end to their journey, but got no answer.

Eventually they emerged into a flattened area — a narrow plateau jutting out of the valley side — that was virtually obscured from all vantage points — not exactly the kind of place a passing traveller might just stumble on — and consisted of nothing but a group of shacks assembled on either side of a rough track.

'Water your hoss for a dollar, mister,' she volunteered when they reached the start of the crude thoroughfare. 'I know about hosses,' she added, with a touch of pride.

Catfoot was tired; so was his horse. He looked at her. 'So you live here.'

'Yeah.'

'And where's your place?'

She pointed to the left of the drag, which was more of a haphazard gap between the shacks than a street. 'Second building along. See, we got a stable. Got a couple of horses too.'

'Horses? Then you got grain?'

'Yeah.'

He walked to the ramshackle stable, checked the interior. There were horses in the stalls as she had mentioned. He nodded a 'hi' to a young man repairing a bridle. The fellow scrutinized him with one eye, his other obscured by a leather patch, and grunted something indecipherable.

With the single eye maintaining its piercing watch on him, Catfoot turned to the girl. 'Well, if you rub him down and feed him,' he said, tossing a coin to her, 'there's another dollar in it for you.'

'It's a deal, mister,' she said, taking the reins.

'Just don't touch his left thigh,' he said. 'He's kinda touchy there.'

He pulled his Winchester from the saddle boot and watched her lead the animal into the building. He threw a friendly gesture, which was unreturned, towards the young man before he resumed his trudge along the unevenly rutted thoroughfare. Even if passing travellers couldn't see this place, he thought, surely they could smell it. Filthy-looking chickens roamed freely all over the place while the track itself was manure-strewn. He could see

— and smell — the bloody remains of a pig's carcass hanging inside a shack.

Further along he noted an old man sitting in a rocking chair on the stoop of a log-house. Bald-headed and thick-necked, the fellow sported tattoos on brawny shoulders. Arms folded and smoking a rough-hewn cherrywood pipe, he appraised the stranger.

Catfoot nodded in greeting but, getting no response, moved on to pass stinking pig sties. As he progressed, the place didn't improve; no more than a clutch of shanties, unpainted and weatherworn. He stepped under a crudely painted sign indicating it was a saloon.

He worked his way around the goat that was tethered at the entrance and entered. The floor was hard-packed earth and the bar was a rough plank on trestles. Catfoot gave a 'hi' to the two occupants. There was no apparent bartender and the seated customers didn't have a smile between them.

'Can a guy get a drink here?' he

asked in as friendly a way as he could muster.

One of the men, who sported a huge grimy sombrero and was chomping on a hunk of bread, threw a glance at the door behind the bar and shouted, 'Charley!'

When Charley eventually appeared it began to strike Catfoot that there was a sameness to the features of folks in town. The bartender, the seated guys, the old man he had seen outside. The same bulbous lips, the small pointed ears.

'Yeah?' the man grunted.

'I'd sure appreciate a beer,' Catfoot said, placing his Winchester on the counter.

The man nodded at the few bottles on a shelf. 'If you can see any beer tell me. That's all we got, feller.'

They were all liquors while Catfoot was in need of a long drink. 'Whiskey,' he said, in the belief that anything was better than nothing.

The man poured him a shot from a

bottle that, like its companions on the shelf, clearly showed it to be homemade hooch.

Catfoot paid and threw back the drink in one, stifling the grimace he felt like displaying as it hit the back of his throat and burned its way down.

The bartender smiled. 'We use it for everything, don't we, boys? From delousing sheep to stripping paint.'

'I feel thirsty,' Catfoot said. 'I'll take another one if I may.'

He'd just taken the second when there was a clump of feet at the door and someone behind him growled, 'What you asking questions for?'

He turned. It was the youngster from the stable with the patch, and the same piggy ears.

'Yeah,' the lad went on, 'I'm talking to you.'

'I ain't asking questions,' Catfoot said. 'Just come in to slake my thirst is all.'

'The fellow's being nosy, boys,' the fellow continued. He gestured towards the stranger. 'You — what's the idea?'

'I got no ideas,' Catfoot said, then glanced around the room as he heard the other two rising from their chairs. 'And I ain't looking for trouble.'

When the three began to move in on him, he knew he wasn't going to able to talk his way out of this. One of his hands regained the Winchester and the other went for his Army Colt. But he'd only partly drawn the weapon when iron fingers gripped his arms from behind. They belonged to the bartender.

One of the customers wrenched the Winchester from him while another grabbed his wrist, the action causing his trigger finger to tighten. Without his intention the pistol banged, putting a slug into the floor. The weapon was yanked from his hand and slung across the room while the strong hands from behind him pulled inwards, constricting his chest.

'Hey, the bozo's trying to kill us,' the sombrero said.

'That went off by accident while I

was trying to defend myself,' Catfoot wheezed. 'Hell, I don't know what's going on. I'm just passing through and, like I said, I ain't looking for trouble.'

'Huh, so you think you can just pass through?' the patch said. 'As easy as that?'

Then a hard bulk crashed against him, driving him sideways. Pain flamed through his rib cage where the bones had crunched against the hard edge of the bar. He fought to keep his balance but a granite-like fist came from the other side, sending him down to the rough planked floor.

Between the man's legs he could see the girl coming into the doorway — and he guessed where they had got the story about him asking questions.

He was hauled to his feet with his arms pinned once more to his sides. The patch walked in front of him and contemplated Catfoot's features while he rubbed his knuckles in anticipation. 'No sir. You ain't passing through just like that — not until we've had a bit of fun. Eh, boys?' And his fist shot straight across Catfoot's jaw. Before the second one came Catfoot could taste blood in his mouth. A couple to his stomach took all the wind from him and he was allowed to drop to the floor.

Dazed and gasping for breath, he felt hands going through his pockets.

'Got us a nice little haul here, boys,' one said eventually, looking at the money stacked on the bar. And he sniggered weirdly.

Catfoot should have known. An out-of-the way place like this, off the beaten track. It wasn't the first time he'd run into a town with no law. In fact, more a straddle of lean-tos than a town. The warning sign should have been when he didn't see a law office on his first appraisal. Such places were natural havens for folk who didn't want anybody nosing into their activities. He should have been more careful — even better, given it a miss altogether.

'Hey, *you* can read,' one said to another.

'This badge and papers — what they say?'

'Huh, the pissant's a lawman. These are Pinkerton papers and badge.'

'Lawman?' someone sneered. 'That means we gotta treat him with respect.'

'Yeah, like this.' And a boot crashed into Catfoot's already tender ribs to the sound of inane giggling. Another boot thudded into his forehead dazing him even further.

'Did he ride in?'

'Yeah,' the patch said, picking up the Winchester and eyeing it covetously.

'If you're having the Winchester, can I have his hoss and saddle?'

'No!' came a thunderous boom. 'We ain't playing finders-keepers.' Through a haze of red, Catfoot looked at the doorway from whence the voice had come. It was the tattooed prize-fighter whom he had seen earlier, cherrywood still clenched between stained teeth. But now the fellow's arms were at his sides — and the large sagging bulges of breasts that were revealed showed the 'fellow' was in fact a woman!

She strode forward and the men cowered away from her. 'Hell, I can't leave you boys out of my sight for more than five minutes without you acting like crazy kids!'

She looked him over, then glanced at his identification papers. 'You're all as stupid as your old man,' she continued, 'which is why I have thanked the Lord every day since he cleared out.'

From her reprimanding tone and general demeanour Catfoot thought for a moment she would be a source of salvation. But when she said, 'This must be the feller,' he guessed the case was otherwise

'What do you mean — the feller?' Catfoot asked. 'You expecting me or som-at?'

Through a blur Catfoot saw the punch coming and tried to ride it. But his neck muscles would not respond to his wish and the woman's hard knuckles smashed into his mouth. He'd never been hit by a woman before and never dreamed it could feel like being smashed with a rock.

'Only speak when you're spoke to,' she snapped by way of explanation. 'Hell, seems like you been causing nothing but trouble since you came in.'

Interrupted by low groans of pain, Catfoot's breathing was coming ragged and heavy. 'Huh,' he grunted. 'Ain't been here long enough to do anything, never mind cause trouble.'

And he knew his ordeal was not over when she added, 'Throw him in a corner and keep your eye on him while I figure out how we're gonna handle this.'

Handle what? There was something about this he didn't understand.

A couple moved eagerly forward, slipped hands under the stranger and jerked him to his feet. Winded and stunned, Catfoot hung limply between the two men as they crossed the room and dropped him to the floor.

Slumped at the end of the room, his brain began to clear and he realized why these folk had the same features. He didn't have to be a Pinkerton detective to see that the town was nothing more than an extended family.

For a while there was silence while the group washed more home-made hooch down their throats. Bad sign. If they were prepared to beat him up when they were relatively sober, what would they be capable of when the juice started to kick in?

Eventually the woman pulled a chair across the room and dropped in front of Catfoot. She straddled it, beefy legs wide apart, and leant on the back to study him through increasingly bleary eyes.

'I apologise for your treatment, mister. See, we don't get many people out here and we all get kinda excited when a stranger rolls up.'

Catfoot had seen enough not to be taken in by the sudden confiding tone. It was just the booze. Like a lull before the next outburst.

'Mind, they can't help it,' she went

on. 'Fact is, their old man was my brother. I know it says in the Bible you shouldn't marry kin but out here there ain't many folks to choose from and we got carried away by our passion.' She laughed and took another swig from the bottle. 'Huh, got carried away with passion several times. Anyways, their pa wasn't troubled by our bedding down together but, I have to admit, it fretted me some. I'd heard it wasn't supposed to be good, a family fornicating amongst itself. But I didn't think it would matter, seeing we hadn't actually sanctified our marriage in church. So, I thought the good Lord might overlook us out here — but he didn't and saw to it that I spawned imbeciles.'

Catfoot glanced at the girl who was standing close. It was clear she didn't share the same looks.

The woman read in his eyes what he was thinking. 'Yeah,' she continued. 'Imbeciles — save for Bunny here.' She stroked the girl's head. 'She's got her marbles. Or most of 'em, ain't you, gal?'

The girl pulled away.

The woman nodded in the direction of his papers. 'Now, we don't cotton to law or Pinkerton men. We're very wary of guys asking questions round here. And I won't insult your intelligence by explaining why.'

He could guess. With the possible exception of the girl, the settlement's inhabitants didn't seem to have more than one brain between them and would be incapable of doing more than scratching a simple living. But the place being at least fifty miles from anything civilized, it was likely they provided holing-up facilities for outlaws on the run. A service for which fugitive outlaws would be willing to pay a fair piece of change. Which explained their antipathy to an inquisitive stranger.

'So, Mr Pinkerton man, why are you on the trail of the pair that came through yesterday?'

'What are you talking about?'

'Credit me with something in my own head, mister. Bunny said you'd been asking about them.'

'Did the couple get the same treatment as me?'

'I told you we don't like questions!' she snarled, and he felt her hard knuckles against his cheekbone. She rubbed her bald pate and, as she took another drink, her demeanour softened. 'In the circumstances, I'll allow you that. No, the boys were out hunting. The pair were in and out before anyone had much chance to take stock.'

Sensible of them, Catfoot thought.

During the interchange the tension had lessened again. But he recognized it as no more than another temporary lull, triggered by the booze.

He realized that when the woman stood up. 'OK, boys,' she said. 'We'll do this thing properly. Set him on a chair and let's get this thing going.'

What thing? Catfoot wondered.

Some answer to his question was given when Sombrero said excitedly, 'We gonna play trials, Ma?'

Catfoot pulled himself into a sitting position and glanced around the room. 'What do you mean — play trials?'

'Damn you,' Patch said. 'You heard Ma. You don't speak unless you're spoken to.'

With that the man turned the Winchester and, with his teeth bared in a snarl, swung the weapon. The butt caught Catfoot under the left ear and he went over sideways with a deep-throated grunt.

11

When Catfoot came to he was roped to a chair in the middle of the room. A tattered Stars and Stripes had been pinned to the far wall before which there was a table and chair. The one with the sombrero was taking bites from a hunk of bread in between swigs of a bottle.

The one with the patch stood at Catfoot's side while another man was drumming his fingers on a table. Suddenly a door opened and the woman staggered in, bottle in hand. She was accompanied by the last son who proclaimed, 'Court be upstanding.'

The man at the table rose while the one beside Catfoot grunted, 'And that means you.'

'How can I stand when I'm roped to a chair, you idiot?'

The man cuffed him.

'Silence in court,' the woman bellowed. She dropped a pencil and paper on the table as she passed. 'That's to make it official.'

The man looked blank. 'What shall I write, Ma?'

'Write your name if you can't manage anything else,' she said. 'Jehosophat, I've laboured enough to teach you how to write that, ain't I?'

'Why should I write my name, Ma?'

She exhaled noisily in frustration and grunted, 'In case you forget it before the end of the trial,' and dropped onto a chair at the head of the room with the flag behind her.

Catfoot might have found the proceedings amusing had it not been for his gut feeling that there could be very serious implications to the weird tableau that was being played out before him.

'Bailiff, read the charge,' the woman instructed the fellow nearest to her.

'What's that mean, Ma?'

'Tell the court what the prisoner is charged with!'

'I don't know, Ma.'

'Do I have to do all this myself?' the woman snapped. She turned her glare to Catfoot. 'The first of the charges is disturbing the peace. How do you plead?'

Catfoot adopted a blank expression. 'Disturbing the peace? What the hell does that mean?'

'You came into our community without invitation. That constitutes breaking the peace.'

Catfoot grunted in disbelief. 'I'm a visitor, if that's what you mean.'

'Were you invited?'

'No.'

'That's it. Now, call the first witness.'

Sombrero took a swig from his bottle, stood up and moved forward. He still had a large hunk of buttered bread in his hand.

'Take off your hat,' Queenie said. She put on some spectacles and stared hard at the man as he removed the sombrero. 'Give your evidence and try not to speak with your mouth full.'

The man kept shifting from one foot to another, looking uneasily at Queenie.

'Give your evidence,' she repeated angrily.

'Well, Ma — '

'For hell's sake, you address me as 'Your honour'. You know that.'

'Well, your honour, this pissant — '

'He might be a pissant but you must refer to him as the defendant. We gotta keep this proper.'

'The defendant rode in yesterday without so much as a by your leave.'

'It's a free country,' Catfoot interjected.

'Number one, it ain't a free country,' the woman said. 'That's just propaganda put about by politicians and schoolteachers and such. Number two, you spoke without being asked to, that constitutes another charge, namely contempt of court. Carry on.'

'Well, Ma — your honour — he asked nobody's permission,' Sombrero said. 'Just came right on in.'

'Did he come in quiet?'

'Quiet?'

The one with the patch raised his hand. 'I could hear his harnesses and horse's hoofs.'

'In my book that constitutes noise,' the woman concluded.

Catfoot shook his head at the craziness of it all.

The woman returned her attention to Sombrero. 'And when he came into our drinking parlour here, did he speak?'

'Yes, your honour. Came right in and started talking.'

'I said 'howdy' for Chrissakes,' Catfoot put in.

She ignored him and concluded, 'OK, guilty on the first charge: that of breaking the peace. What's the second charge?'

After some seconds of silence, the woman harrumphed in frustration. 'Discharging the contents of a pistol within the town precincts, that's what,' she said. 'How do you plead?'

'Hell, it was an accident,' Catfoot replied.

'Nevertheless, you were the perpetrator. So that's settled — guilty. Now what's the third charge?'

The men looked blank. She grunted in irritation, jabbing a finger at Catfoot's identification papers and badge on the table before her. 'Conducting yourself under false pretences. How do you plead?'

'This is the height of stupidity,' Catfoot said.

'Are you not some kind of agent?'

'You know that. You got my identification documents in front of you.'

'Yes,' Queenie said. 'That brings us to the documents. Call the next witness.'

The bartender stood forward.

'And what was your part in this?' she asked.

'When that badge and set of papers were found on him, it was me that read 'em, your honour.'

'And what did these items indicate?'

'That the guy is a Pinkie.'

'What does that mean — a Pinkie?'

'A Pinkerton detective. Hell, Ma, you know that.'

'Had he disclosed this fact prior to

your searching him?'

'No, Ma.'

Queenie looked across at Catfoot. 'Did you disclose that you were a Pinkerton agent before they searched you?'

'No. There was no need, and it's not a crime.'

'The court decides what is a crime!'

She ruminated, then said, 'That you entered the community without declaring yourself signifies you must have meant some mischief, or else you would have revealed your identity like an honest man. So, the accused admits the subterfuge — that proves without a shadow of a doubt that he is guilty on the third charge.'

'It doesn't prove anything of the sort,' Catfoot said.

'I will ignore that interruption, itself another contempt of court. As for a fourth charge, the contempt of court we noted previously, that has already been handled so we now have a summary — guilty on all four charges.'

She stared at Catfoot. 'Have you anything to say before sentence is passed?'

'None of the things you've cited are crimes. And this is not a court.'

She ignored his observations. 'The guilty shall rise to receive the verdict of the court.'

'I can't rise. I'm tied to a chair, goddamnit.'

'Very well, I'll allow you to take the verdict while sitting. Either way it makes no difference. The verdict is you shall be taken from this place and hung by the neck until you are dead.'

Catfoot had sensed this whole thing was heading in an ominous direction. Now he knew. 'If you carry this out,' he mouthed, 'you'll all be guilty of murder.'

The woman laughed. 'How little you know.'

'And you dishonour that flag behind you.'

She rose and grabbed a corner of the flag. 'This?' she scoffed, and tore it from the wall. 'Here we have our own honour — and law.'

She rose and strode towards the door. 'Bring the varmint outside so that sentence can be carried out.'

'But he's tied to the chair, Ma.'

'Then re-rope him!'

Charley looked at Sombrero. 'Give me a hand.'

The big man grabbed hold of Catfoot's shoulders while the other untied the ropes.

'Now stand and stick your hands out.'

Eventually Catfoot was pushed towards the daylight.

12

They dragged him outside and pushed him along the main track to where he could see his horse tethered in the distance.

'You'll regret this,' he said. 'You're not just dealing with the law here; you're dealing with the Pinkerton Agency. They never give up.'

The woman grunted. 'They'll never find this place, never mind your body.'

'No,' Sombrero said with a laugh, his hat now back in place. 'That'll provide pig fodder for a couple of days. Then — nothing!'

Catfoot was suddenly aware of the pigs grunting, as though they had understood. He was pushed towards a tree with branches that spewed over the track. Then one of the men came forward, leading his palomino. Seemingly from nowhere there appeared a large canvas bag, which tied up at the mouth with strings. Into this they rammed Catfoot's head. He felt a noose pulled round his neck. Then strong hands heaved him up and into the saddle.

'Throw the rope over the branch,' the woman shouted.

He could tell by the sounds that it took several attempts before the rope was satisfactorily thrown into place With bladders full of hooch none of them were competent and their bungling gave him time to think. Then he remembered the warning he had been given about the horse's tender flank.

Thankfully the idiot who had tied his hands had thoughtlessly tied them in front. Catfoot thrust his hands forward, locking them around the pommel, and jammed his left foot backwards into the horse's thigh. The animal snorted and reared. For a few seconds, it snickered and pawed the air with its rider fighting to stay in the saddle. Around him the would-be executioners shouted.

Then the mass of agitated horseflesh sprang forward. Instinctively Catfoot allowed the horse its head, hoping it would have the inclination to continue its headlong rush.

'After him!' he heard the woman shout.

It would take them a little time to get astride their own horses, so if he could stay in the saddle he stood some chance. Maybe his action was just delaying the inevitable, but a condemned man will go for any chance, no matter how remote.

★ ★ ★

He was a long distance from the hanging tree and hadn't heard any noise behind him for some time. But still he goaded the animal on.

Suddenly the horse jumped over some obstacle. Catfoot came down heavily into the saddle losing his balance. He could feel himself slipping obliquely and finally he hit the ground, striking his head on something hard in the process. And then all went blank.

* * *

He didn't know how long he lay unconscious. What he did know was he came to sensing someone fiddling with the drawstrings of the bag over his head.

He grunted and tried to lash out with his still-tied fists.

'Don't worry. Everything's all right.' It was a young, female voice. When the bag was slipped off it was dark but he could make out the face of the girl known as Bunny.

'It's lucky I found you,' she said. 'I've been looking for a long time.'

He whirled his aching head around. 'Where are the others?'

'No need to fear,' she said, as she began picking at the knots of the binding round his wrists. 'They've given up looking for you for the time being. They're a long ways off now.'

When his hands were free he fingered the bump on his head and winced. He explored his tender ribs and wheezed again.

'So you're safe for the moment,' she went on. 'Now the question is where to take you for safety.'

He tried to rise but still felt too woozy to stand. 'I don't understand why you're concerned. You're one of them.'

'No, I'm not one of them, especially after what I've learned today.'

'You seen my horse?'

'No. I think he's got the sense to get as far away from that horrible place as possible.' She glanced around. 'And we should do the same. Even though I guess there's no immediate danger, I figure they'll come looking again at first light.'

She wiped his forehead with a handkerchief. 'So, let me know when you think you can start walking.'

'OK,' he said, and lay back for a little more respite. Then: 'I don't understand why you're helping me.'

'I felt guilty for having led you to them. Believe me, when I did so I didn't know what they intended. Then, when I could see what was happening — that silly trial thing — I wanted to help but didn't see what I could do. I felt terrible and utterly helpless while they played their stupid game. But when they chased after you I found myself alone. I knew there was little chance of me being able to help but I had to follow just in case.'

She waved an arm upwards. 'I kept to the ridge up there so they wouldn't see me. When it got dark they headed back home, but I carried on. And then eventually I found you here in the undergrowth.'

He left it for another couple of minutes. 'OK, I'm ready to move.'

She helped him to his feet.

Besides the bump to his head and sore ribs, his body was aching from the fall.

'We'd better continue in this direction,' she said. 'At least it's away from the Place.'

Having been sightless for God-knows how long, he was disorientated. 'Have we come in the direction in which I first came?'

'Yes.'

'Good. Further on there's an old man's shack. It's back quite a stretch, but if we can reach it, we can rest up there.'

'How do you know about it?'

'I came across it on the way here.'

'This old man, can you trust him?' she asked.

'The place is probably empty. But if he returns, I'm sure he'll allow us shelter. He seemed an amiable fellow.'

And they began their trek.

★ ★ ★

'You live with them back there?' he asked after they had gone some way.

'Yes.'

'You don't have their looks. Are you one of the family?'

'No. I ain't a Rawlings.'

152

'So that's their name. Ma Rawlings and her boys.'

'Yes.'

'So what were you doing there?'

'Some time back my pa and I were travelling this way. We were lost and stumbled on the Place. He wasn't very well and asked for shelter for the both of us. We stayed the night but in the morning he was gone. Queenie said he'd gone on ahead. Being ill he didn't want to be a burden to me, that's what she told me. They couldn't stop him from leaving they said. I had to stay because I had no money. At first they seemed kind but then bad things started to happen.'

'What bad things?'

She didn't answer immediately, then continued in a low voice. 'The young men started taking me to their bed. Sometimes all of them at the same time. There was nothing I could do about it.'

'Jesus,' he muttered. Then: 'Didn't you try to get away?'

She screwed up her face at the thought. 'Yes, once. They caught me and brung me back. Kept me locked up for a couple of days in the dark in my own filth and with no food. Said that if I tried to escape again they would feed me to the hogs. Like they were threatening to do to you.'

'And you haven't seen your father since?'

'No. And I don't think things happened like they say. You see, Pa was a religious man and wore a small golden crucifix around his neck. I've noticed that Queenie now wears such a pendant.'

'So you don't think he left as they'd said?'

'I didn't really think so from the start. He wouldn't have left me like that.'

'So what do you think happened?'

'I think they killed him, kept his few belongings and fed him to the hogs.'

'What makes you think that?'

'From snippets of conversation I've

overheard during my stay there, it seems they make a living out of preying on passing strangers.'

'The desolate hell-hole that it is, you may be right. I've heard of such places before.'

She shuddered and added, 'I think they use the pigs to dispose of the bodies.'

He nodded. 'You said you regretted leading me there. Why did you?'

'Queenie just told me to. I didn't know why at the time. But from what I've been able to piece together today, I'm beginning to understand. See, a man and woman passed through yesterday.'

'Yes, you mentioned them.'

'Anyways, what I've overheard since, it seems the guy gave them money to prevent you following them.'

Catfoot shook his head at the revelation. He'd reckoned he'd been tailing the couple unseen, but it was now clear they must have sighted him some time.

'So, I ain't as clever as I thought,' he said. Then he went on: 'If this guy was handing out money it must have occurred to them there could be a deal more. Why didn't they kill him and take it?'

'The boys were out hunting when the couple turned up so there was only Queenie and me. The stranger carried a heavy hand pistol and a rifle. Tough as the old woman is, I figure that was too much for her by herself. She invited them to stay over — I figure with the intention of waiting for the boys to come back so they could handle him — but the pair took some refreshment, the fellow struck his deal and they left.'

Suddenly Catfoot stopped. 'Quiet,' he whispered. 'I saw movement in the darkness over there, by that tree. You stay here.'

He edged forward, and eventually made out the shape of a horse. As he approached he relaxed, recognizing the palomino. Up close he stroked the horse's muzzle. 'You sure deserve your name. You did a good job, Buck. Come on, you're with friends now.'

He led the horse down to the bottom of the valley and they resumed their journey.

★   ★   ★

Dawn was breaking when they sighted the shack. The old man had not yet returned and they made themselves at home.

As he was resting, Bunny examined his head. 'There's some blood. Needs attention.'

He took a blotchy mirror from the wall and had a look for himself. 'Another one to add to the collection,' he said, noting the bruising to his face.

After the girl had bathed the wound, he cleaned up and set to making breakfast from the ample stores. The food was good and went a long way to filling his empty belly.

The girl straightened the bed and patted it. 'You need sleep.'

He shook his head. 'You get on it. You need rest and sleep.'

He lowered himself onto a bearskin on the floor. 'I'll rest for a spell, but only to get a second wind. I ain't sleeping. I have things to do.'

'Such as what?' she asked as she eased herself onto the bed.

'My first intention is to put a satisfactory end to a certain matter.'

'You mean the couple you are chasing.'

'No, that comes second.'

13

Bunny was still sleeping when he left the cabin. He'd scoured the place, coming up with two early model hand pistols — a Dragoon and a Remington — and a hunting rifle. He had cleaned them, checked them over, but refrained from testing them lest the shots were overheard.

Then he'd headed back towards the Place keeping away from the main track. He was whacked but rage fuelled his body making up for tiredness. If Bunny had been right, the crazies would be heading this way again so his horse wouldn't have to haul him the whole way back. Every now and then he would stop and listen. Eventually he heard the faintest of noises ahead. He dismounted, tethered his horse and cautiously picked his way down.

He stopped again when he heard

voices. Not too far away.

'You think he got this far, Ma?'

'Just keep quiet and keep looking.'

Catfoot saw them spread out along the valley floor and he took cover behind a tree. Each had a gun while the woman had her filthy hand clasped around his Army Colt. He waited until they were nearer, then stepped out so that he would be in view but keeping close to the tree in case he needed its cover.

'You looking for me?' he yelled.

'It's the Pinky!' one of the men shouted.

The woman nodded her head by way of instruction and they fanned out further across the valley floor.

As they raised their guns, Catfoot hurled himself to the ground, simultaneously squeezing the triggers of the old man's pistols.

The borrowed guns worked and two of the Rawlings went down from the first shots out of them, one dead, the other writhing with a dose of lead in his stomach. Two others only managed to loose off a few rounds while Catfoot's guns barked repeatedly.

The last standing figure was the woman but she took a bullet in the throat. For a moment she stood motionless, then toppled backwards.

He approached the figure of the gut-shot man, now folded tight in a foetal position. He turned the man's head with the barrel-end of his rifle and was met by open but lifeless eyes.

He strolled over to the woman. She was still alive, blood frothing from her mouth and more oozing from the hole in her throat.

He retrieved his Army Colt which had fallen from her hand. 'I hope you ain't damaged Old Faithful here.' He checked it over before slipping it into his holster. Then he eased the crucifix and chain from around her neck.

She tried to speak but it was just a gurgle.

'Huh,' he grunted. 'You talk a lot about justice. Fact is, there's no way you'll live with that wound. Now *that's* justice.'

Suddenly there was a noise behind him and he whirled round, gun ready to speak again.

It was the girl.

'Hey, Bunny. I hoped you wouldn't follow.'

'I woke up to find you gone and thought maybe you'd need help again.'

He chuckled without humour. 'Not this time. But thanks for the thought.' He handed her the crucifix. 'Here, this is rightfully yours.'

As she slipped it around her neck, he surveyed the carnage. 'Are you bothered by dead people?' he asked.

'No. I seen dead folk, my pa being a minister and all. And I ain't bothered about these especially. It was what they deserved.'

'OK, as you're here, you can give me a hand. Help me collect the weapons and whatever money and valuables they're carrying.'

It wasn't long before he had retrieved

his own weapons. When they had completed the task, Bunny glanced around the scene. 'What about the bodies?'

'They can rot in hell as they are. They don't deserve a Christian burial. Now let's round up their horses.'

★   ★   ★

When they got back to the shack, the old man had returned from his painting the town red. Catfoot recounted the subsequent events and thanked the man for use of his shack and equipment.

'I never went up that way these days,' the man said. 'I was hunting up there once and somebody took a pot-shot at me. On top of that I'd heard rumours of something not right out there. It was only scuttlebutt and I didn't know exactly what was going on. But you and I weren't together long enough for me to think of warning you.'

'I understand. The whole point of

their way of life was that *nobody* knew what was going on.'

'I'm sure sorry I didn't say anything to you.'

'Don't worry, old-timer. Water under the bridge.'

'What you gonna do now?'

'Head back there. It's on my way.' He threw a glance at Bunny. 'And you're coming with me.'

She shook her head. 'I never want to see that place again.'

'So what you gonna do now that you're out of the hell-hole?'

She looked blank. 'Don't know.'

'Exactly,' Catfoot said. 'I understand the place has vile memories for you. But you're a young gal and you've got your future to think of. Of course, the choice is yours but I suggest you come along with me. On the way through we can see what we can salvage. There'll be things of value there. No need to leave stuff for any passing strangers to filch. You need recompensing for what you've lost and what you've gone through.'

The girl still looked blank. 'And what then?'

'We'll play it as it comes.' He looked at the old man. 'I'm gonna take one of the horses as a pack horse and one for the girl. You can have the other two. Same with the armoury.'

They rested with a final coffee, then made preparations for leaving. Just before they mounted up the old man handed Catfoot a package of food he had prepared for their journey. 'That should see you through a few miles.'

'Obliged,' Catfoot said. After he had fixed it in a saddle-bag, he took some bills and coins from his pocket and handed them over. 'And that's for allowing me use of your place.'

He helped the girl into the saddle, then hauled himself into his own. He leant down to shake the old man's hand. 'Thanks again. You gonna be OK?'

'Sure thing.'

'And what you gonna do now?'

The old man looked at his new stock

of horses. 'Have a rest-up then head back to Low Water Creek. I got some selling to do.'

Catfoot chuckled. 'Hell, twice in one week? I hope you don't take it as discourteous if I say you're not a young buck anymore. Just don't overdo it with those women back there.'

The old man returned the chuckle. 'Thanks for the warning but, if it comes to it, what a way to die, eh?'

★ ★ ★

In dazzling sunlight the conglomeration known as the Place still looked evil. Even the grunting of the pigs, normally a natural sound, now had ominous tones.

'OK,' he said, dropping down from his horse. 'You start at one end of the town and I'll move in from the other. We're looking for money, loot and anything of value. You might have a better idea of the whereabouts of hidey-holes than me.'

An hour later they had cash, jewellery, a few more guns and a variety of knives and other tools.

'We can't take it all,' he said, appraising the haul, 'especially the heavy stuff. We'll pick the most valuable and load up the trail horse. We should get something from trading in the next town.'

From the money they had found he took a cut for travel spending and handed the bulk to the girl.

'I can't take all that,' she said.

'You can and you will.'

'But *you* deserve more for bringing an end to it all.'

'No. What I did to the Rawlings was personal. Not to mention payback time for your father and countless others who might have been unfortunate enough to fall into their clutches.'

'What about the livestock?'

'We'll set them free. At least they'll have some chance in the wild. Try to shoo them away from the Place.'

When that task was completed, he

assembled the horses some distance away ready to resume their journey.

'Well, that's it,' he said, turning to survey the ramshackle settlement. 'We've salvaged all we can. Just one more job to do.'

In his search of the place he had noticed a tar barrel. He took an axe from a store and chopped some wood, paying special attention to cutting some into a variety of thin laths. He built a small fire in the middle of the track. When it was in full blaze he soaked the end of the laths in tar and touched them to the fire. He told the girl to do her best to ensure no animals returned, then he toured the settlement throwing burning brands through doors and windows.

When he had satisfied himself that the fire had got a good grip on every building he joined the girl and took a final look at the scene before mounting up.

Without glancing back, he turned his horse and heeled it up to an easy canter, the girl falling into line behind him.

14

It was early afternoon when they rode into a settlement proclaiming itself to be Panhandle City. He found a clean looking boarding house and took rooms.

'I'm sorry this episode has lost you some time in your pursuit,' Bunny said, after they had taken some mouthfuls of food at the table in the dining room.

'Can't be helped. Besides, I've learned a few things.'

'Such as?'

'This guy knows I'm on his trail. And he's taking me seriously. He proved that when he showed he was willing to hand out cash to get Queenie and her mob to stall me.'

'But it's cost you time.'

'That's true. I've lost a couple of days. That reminds me. When the couple turned up at the Rawlings' place, there was only you and the old woman there. Did you see anything of these folk? The man in particular, can you tell me anything about him?'

'Queenie did all the talking. I stayed in the background. I only saw them at a distance. I can tell you what the gal looked like — '

'I know about her.'

'But the feller . . . all I can say is he was solid-built. Think I caught sight of some sideburns. That's about all.'

She screwed up her face in an effort to recall. 'Oh, and his gun,' she added. 'Now I remember. Had the look of a Beaumont-Adams. You know, one of them solid-frame jobs.'

'You can't give me much on his appearance yet you can describe his gun?'

'I caught a brief sight of him through the window. He was checking the gun while the animals were drinking.'

He looked perplexed. 'OK, but how come a young slip of a girl, a reverend's daughter to boot, can identify the make of a pistol?'

'It stuck in my mind 'cos my old

grandpa brung one back from the war just like it. Was always cleaning it and talking about the old days.'

'Beamont-Adams, eh? Don't see many of them. Thanks. Every little helps and that's a little extra.' He looked out of the window. 'Well, there's still time left in the day for me to find out if anyone's seen anything of the pair.'

★ ★ ★

It was dark; candles were guttering in shop windows as he neared the end of completing his tour of the town's boarding establishments. He had only a few establishments left at which to make inquiries when he struck lucky. A proprietor at one place recognized his description of the couple. 'And I'm glad they've gone.'

'Why?'

The man raised his nose in the air. 'Can you smell that?'

'No. Maybe a whiff of carbolic.'

'More than that. Hell, *I* can still smell it. It permeated the place. See, they had quite a problem. They'd gone down with something. If I'd known the exactness of it I would have sent them elsewhere. Leastways we had no other guests at the time. Whatever they'd got, it kept them in bed for two days. Complained of headaches and stomach pains but it was the loose bowels that gave *us* the problem. Doc says it must have been something they'd eaten. There was a hell of a smell in the room and it began permeating through the whole place. Huh, it was a day before they could take anything to eat. Then the missus took soup up to them; it was all they could face.'

'Where are they now?'

'Praise be to the Lord, they checked out this afternoon.'

This afternoon! Catfoot was almost on their tail again. 'You know which way they headed out?'

'I figure so. They asked for the

nearest railroad. I told them Stainesville.'

'How far is that?'

'About a day's ride north.'

'You got a map?'

'No.'

'Not to mind, you've been helpful
enough. Thanks.'

Catfoot identified himself to the
sheriff where there was a map on the
law office wall from which he worked
out a route to the depot.

★　★　★

Back at the boarding house he had a
question for Bunny. 'You know when
you told me that Queenie supplied the
renegade couple with refreshment?
What did she feed them?'

'Oh, that. There was a side of pork in
the store.' She laughed at the memory.
'She and her sons didn't know that it
had gone off until one of the boys took
a chunk of it and ended up on the john
for a couple of days. They were a dirty

bunch; never got rid of anything. Left it hanging up.'

'Yeah,' he said. 'I remember it.'

'Well, when the visitors turned up and the boys weren't around, like I told you, it looked like they were going to escape Queenie's clutches. So she served it to them during their short stay. But it didn't work.'

He chuckled. 'It did, and it caught up with them! Just took its time is all. Huh, they've been confined to their room and haven't been able to leave town until today. That means I'm within striking distance again.'

'When are you leaving?'

'It's too late now. It'll have to be first thing in the morning.' He thought for a moment. 'That'll give me time to see to one more thing.'

'What's that?'

'I can't rightly leave this place until I've got you fixed up somewhere. Now, clean yourself up and comb your hair. We've got someone to see.'

'What's it all about?'

He explained about a notice that had caught his eye while he'd been making his inquiries about town.

★ ★ ★

The town doctor was just about to close his surgery when Catfoot knocked on the door.

'Your notice about wanting an assistant,' he said, after introductions had been made. 'I think this young lady fits the bill.'

Inside, the doctor explained how his wife had helped him in his job but she had recently died after a short illness. 'As fit as a fiddle,' he said, 'and had a simple fall. There was nothing wrong with her except pain. She didn't appear to have any bones broken. Just needed rest and something to kill the pain. But once she was in bed she succumbed to one infection after another.' He stared at the floor for a moment. 'Huh, a doctor — and I couldn't save my own wife.'

'These things happen,' Catfoot said

softly. 'I'm sure you did your best.'

After a while the doctor perked up. 'So this young lady sees herself as a nurse, does she?'

Catfoot took off his hat and showed the wound to his head, then indicated his varied nicks and abrasions. 'Had a spot of trouble a-ways back. This young lady cleaned up the damage. She's got experience all right. So, if you'll give her a try, sir.'

'Might do, let's see. Can you read and write?'

'Yes, sir.'

'Her pa was a reverend,' Catfoot added.

'Ha, from professional stock, eh?' the doctor observed. 'Good. That means you can help with records and correspondence as my wife did.'

After a few more questions from both sides, an agreement was reached.

★ ★ ★

'Before I leave,' Catfoot said to Bunny when they were back in the hotel, 'we'll get your money into a bank.'

He opened the dresser drawer and took out the bag of jewellery and other trinkets of value that they had collected. 'The money and this stuff will give you something to fall back on. And your job with the doctor will give you some purpose and allow you time to decide if it's what you want. If not, you'll have the grubstake to move on.'

She looked out of the window. 'Looks like a good town with nice folk.'

'Sure does. You could do worse. This is an established community serving farming needs. Quiet and respectable, not as wild and woolly as a cowtown, believe me.'

15

The trail — often less than a path — was difficult to make out and Catfoot had to concentrate to follow it as it wended slowly out of the valleys. It was some miles on that he hit a more established trail and his mind was able to turn to evaluating his recent experience. The upshot was he had some physical description of the man — vague but better than nothing. And he knew the type of gun he carried. That could be a relevant fact in helping to identify the guy if ever he should catch up with him. The Beaumont-Adams was a rare weapon.

And he'd learned that the couple were headed for Stainesville and the railroad. The little bits added up to what could be a useful set of leads.

Then the aches and pains reminded

him he had paid a price for the information. Maybe it had been worth it.

★ ★ ★

Days passed. The sun was getting hotter, the terrain bleaker. But all things have an upside and the sandy soil made prints easier to spot.

Whether it was the passage of time or his focusing on the task in hand he didn't know, but something was gradually tempering the recollection of his unhappy homecoming, helping his mind to adjust to his broken personal life. He mused about the way his attitude towards the wife stealer was changing.

The strange thing was the more he thought about it the less he held it against the man. Adey was a good guy, after all, a friend to both of them. Their affair probably began with him innocently offering company to a lonely woman and things just developed from there. Catfoot was old enough to know that such things could happen without malice. In fact, knowing the man, he wouldn't be surprised if Adey himself was feeling bad about the whole matter. And, as he'd repeatedly told himself, it was his own fault. If he'd given as much thought to his marriage as he gave to chasing varmints, maybe he could have done something about it before it was too late.

Huh, he told himself, if this softening process keeps up he might get to the point, should he meet Adey in the street, when he might as soon as say, 'How you doing, pal?' than smash him in the mouth.

When he crossed the Cimarron on a south-westerly heading, the character of the land became noticeably rockier and the terrain took on a permanent upward gradient, calling for more rest-ups.

★ ★ ★

In time he topped one of the interminable rises to hear the distant, mournful whistle of a locomotive. He gigged his horse and it wasn't long before he could see smoke rising above a settlement and was soon passing a board proclaiming the town of Stainesville. He kept his speed along main street where he could see the depot at the end with its impatient locomotive and retinue of cars.

Reaching the station building he hitched his horse to the nearest stanchion and leapt up onto the boarding.

'Where's the train bound?' he asked of the ticket man at the booking window.

'Six Shooter Siding. Or Tucumcari to give it its official name in the timetable.'

'You see a man and a woman get on?'

'Sorry, mister, there's thirty passengers or more boarded.'

'Woman got a carpetbag, fellow thickset.'

The man shook his head. 'All passengers look alike to me, sir.'

Catfoot scanned the cars labelled

Rock Island Railroad, six in all. Of course, this didn't have to be the train. He'd made good headway and estimated his prey were no more than a day ahead of him so if they'd caught another he was still only a day behind. But if they'd caught an earlier train they could be heading in either direction. He looked up and down the track. *Which way?*

'How regular are the trains?' he asked.

The man glanced along the lines of metal disappearing over the southeast horizon. 'Ain't much out there, which is why the company have took their time laying track. Ain't been laid long. I ain't been out there myself but I'm told Tucumcari ain't much more than a bunch of tents even now.'

'So?'

'So we don't get many trains. This is the first one in three days.'

If they'd caught a train, this had to be it!

He gave his credentials. 'Mind if I go

aboard and check the passengers?'

'I don't mind at all, sir. But you don't have time. It's running late.' He threw a glance at the Dutch clock on the wall. 'Was due out two minutes ago.'

Catfoot looked up and down the cars lining the track. There were a few folks mounting the steps but there was no sign of the objects of his pursuit. The engineer was leaning out of his cab watching them with an obvious impatience.

Catfoot looked along the platform and noticed a man with a badge leaning back on a chair against the wall.

He loped over to the lawman and showed him his credentials. 'I need to board the train, Sheriff,' he said after introductions and some brief explanation of his situation. 'I ain't got much time so I'd be obliged if you could quarter my horse.' On account of the standing of the Pinkerton Agency, they had a working relationship with public law officers. 'You can telegraph my base at Denver for verification. Either way

I'll get the office to telegraph you about what to do with the animal.'

The man was willing to cooperate and Catfoot returned to the station keeper's window. He bought a ticket and took his belongings from the horse. Then he went to the end of the train and boarded at the observation platform with the intent of working his way methodically through the cars.

He dropped wearily into a seat in the last compartment just as the locomotive gave its final whistle and the train juddered forward with a clanking of couplings.

While the train gathered momentum he surveyed his fellow occupants in the car. In the main he could only see the backs of their heads but he could make out enough to know that none fitted the description of the persons he was looking for.

So, swaying with the motion of the train, he rose and moved down the aisle towards the next car. It proved just as fruitless. At the station he'd counted six cars, so there were four more to go.

He was nearing the end of the fourth when he spied a single girl looking out of the window. He dropped into a vacant seat and studied her as best he could from the rear until he was pretty sure she was Gypsy Jane. But if so, where was her companion? Were they making their train journey separately? Catfoot couldn't think why that would be.

If the man were a villain as Catfoot was now certain, he would keep his eyes peeled as a matter of habit even if he had no reason to suspect they were being pursued anymore. And Catfoot didn't think he had yet been close enough behind them during the last day to have been spotted. Had they separated for some reason at Staines-ville and only the girl had boarded the train?

He looked at the other passengers. He still didn't know with any precision what the mysterious man looked like, but there was no one that might have raised his curiosity, nor was there a single man seated apart.

He dearly wanted to inspect the remaining two cars but the woman knew what he looked like and he needed a way of getting past her without her recognizing him. The opportunity came some ten minutes later when a woman entered behind him and moved down the swaying aisle. He leapt to his feet and kept close to her.

'Not the easiest thing is it, ma'am?' he said. 'Walking on a moving train.'

She glanced back. 'It surely is not.'

When level with the girl he got as near to the woman as he could in the pretence of their being a couple and, continuing meaningless pleasantries, eased past the girl with his back to her. At the end he opened the door for the woman to pass, then he exited behind her.

The woman moved to the next car while he, no longer in need of her cover, remained behind for a moment on the platform.

After a while he crossed over and entered the fifth car. His search was profitless yet again and he'd crossed onto the rear platform of the remaining car when he came face to face with the conductor. He made to enter but the man barred his way saying, 'As I recall, you don't have a ticket for the sleeper, sir.'

He was a short, elderly fellow and would have provided no successful resistance had Catfoot simply pushed his way by. But the resulting kerfuffle would be likely to warn anybody within the car of trouble, so he didn't force himself.

'Sorry, pal. Just stretching my legs and didn't realize this was a sleeping car.' He crossed back to the platform of the adjacent car and yawned. 'How far to the next stop?'

The man looked at his watch. 'Stopping for water and fuel in about an hour, sir.'

'In that case, I'll try and get myself some shut-eye.'

He returned inside the car and dropped into the first available seat. From what he knew of the geography of the territory, the journey itself was going to take the best part of a day, so there was plenty of time for the opportunity to arise for him to check out the sleeper carriage.

He relaxed, pulled his hat partially over his eyes and feigned sleep. It was some time later that he heard the door open. Still maintaining his pretence of being oblivious to his surroundings he noted that it was the old conductor passing back down the train.

When the man had disappeared from the car at the rear end, Catfoot made his way forward to the sleeper. Inside he checked the berths one by one. Nearly all were empty and he excused himself with a quiet 'my mistake' whenever he disturbed the occasional occupant.

In time he found himself on the forward platform behind the fuel tender.

He'd drawn a blank. Had the man

not boarded the train after all? Or had he somehow missed him? But having investigated the length of the train he couldn't see how that could have happened.

He grunted to himself in frustration. Nothing for it but to work back the whole length of the train and recheck.

Eventually he was standing on the rear platform with nothing but moonlit tracks to look at. His irritation resulted in another grunt and he built himself a smoke.

He was in a quandary. The only tangible thing he'd got on this caper now was the girl. But he couldn't arrest her. The only thing he'd got on her was that she had known Bodeen — not a crime in itself. He could question her about her mysterious travelling companion but all she had to do was keep quiet. He could probably get her off the train at the next town and into a law office to question her in more intimidating surroundings. But if she had half a brain she would know all she had to do was remain quiet, and if she had more than half a brain she could sue Pinkerton's for wrongful arrest. That could spell trouble for his standing with the agency, as the trigger for the whole thing was purely speculation on his part.

He was pushing these thoughts around when he sensed a noise above the sounds made by the travelling car. For a moment he couldn't figure out why it was catching his attention. The point was there was a rhythm to the rattle of the car and clangour of wheels on track and, although not louder, the new noise he heard was not part of that rhythm.

He turned in its direction and saw a shape against the moonlit sky — the shape of a figure creeping down the ladder from the top of the car. He caught a glimpse of a gun being drawn as the shadowy form swung round onto the platform.

Catfoot instinctively went for the gun wrist, gripping it with both hands, and for a moment the two figures were locked as muscle tensed against muscle. He managed to wrench the weapon from the man's hand and it clattered onto the platform. But his attacker took the opportunity to crack his fist against Catfoot's temple sending him reeling back against the guardrail.

Catfoot shook his head and he cleared it just in time to see the figure seeking to retrieve the gun. He rammed his boot into the man, knocking him off balance.

As the man sprawled backwards groaning and wheezing for breath, Catfoot leapt on him and, gripping his front, sent a fast succession of short hammer-blows into his face. The man's arms came up, in vain seeking to kill the power behind the punches.

'Right, you bastard!' Catfoot grunted. He drew his arm back in order to deliver a final, incapacitating blow with all his weight behind it.

But something solid hit him on the back of the head, not the hardest of blows but enough to temporarily mute his assault — and enough for the man to wriggle from his grip. Trying simultaneously to stave off the attack from behind and contend with his male attacker was too much and another blow felled him.

He caught a whiff of perfume and knew his new assailant was a woman. It had to be Gypsy Jane. Through his daze he could make out the man now at the other side of the platform, lining up the gun.

Given the distance between them and his semi-stunned condition there was no way he could get out of the line of fire nor have the time to get to the man before he pulled the trigger.

'What's going on there?' came a voice. Muffled, the voice was that of the conductor from inside the car.

The man cursed and sheathed his gun. 'Stall him.'

While the girl went inside to appease the conductor, the big fellow grabbed the still-woozy agent and heaved him over the rail.

Catfoot bounced and slithered down the scree, his already bruised body taking more of a battering.

Seconds later, the man joined the girl inside the car. 'Don't worry, old timer,' he said to the conductor. 'Just joshing around with my girl. We got a bit boisterous is all.' Then he added with a wink, 'You know how it is.'

The conductor only seemed half convinced and put his head round the door to check the platform for himself. He seemed satisfied when he saw nobody.

The couple made their way to their seats and sat down.

'He won't be able to catch up with us now,' the man whispered when the conductor was out of earshot. 'I was hoping to have plugged him.' Then he added with a satisfaction, 'But there's a good chance the fall will have killed him.'

16

He lay at the bottom of the scree, feeling like most of the bones in his body were broken. But when he'd recovered enough of his wind to check, he reckoned he had no serious injury through some miracle. He rolled over and looked in the distance — and he knew what had been the main contribution to his not sustaining grave damage. The train had halted! He could see it now in the distance alongside a water tower. In the heat of the moment something that nobody on that car platform had realized — including he — was that the train had been slowing down. It was the deceleration that had taken the edge off his fall.

He hauled himself to his feet. Maybe bones weren't broken, but bruising and stiffness were certainly making themselves felt. However, setting his sights on re-boarding the train diminished the pain and he heavy-footed along the track as fast as his pummelled body would allow him.

For a while the gap didn't seem to lessen. But eventually he neared the halt, the sound of the steam hissing angrily from the locomotive got louder. He had to get a move on. It was only a brief fuelling and watering stop. The crew had nearly completed their task. He could make out the fireman swinging the hosepipe back towards the water tower and the engineer capping the locomotive's tank.

A whistle blasted.

He tried to run faster but his effort was in vain.

He heard pistons thundering and wheels spinning as they sought traction against the metal rails. He stumbled to the ground and as he hauled himself to his feet he could see the huge locomotive beginning to pull its retinue of cars away from the halt.

He hobbled as fast as he could along

the track but when he was aware that the gap between him and the vehicle was widening inexorably he stopped. Bending forward and panting, he dropped his hands to his knees for support.

His body insisting on, and getting, respite allowed him to make some assessment. The escapade back on the train had revealed several things. Firstly, *they* knew he was still after them. From the time they had high-tailed it out of Dodge they had known it was possible and he must have been sighted on their trail for the fellow to splash out cash for him to be stopped. But they couldn't have known he had got past Queenie and her boys unless they'd seen him again. But how? He was sure they hadn't sighted him again while he was dogging them across country. He had been especially careful. What was more likely was that the girl — who already knew what he looked like — had spied him from the window when he rode into Stainesville. Might even have witnessed his exchange with the sheriff at the depot.

Secondly, he had had confirmation that it was the same fellow who had travelled through the Rawlings' place — because in the set-to on the train he had seen enough of the guy's gun, even in the dark, to identify it as a solid-frame Beaumont-Adams, just like Bunny had said.

And lastly, his suspicions about the background of the mystery man had been given hard foundation. Big Jack Logan, or whoever he was, was prepared to kill to prevent being traced. That meant he was guilty of something bad, and his willingness to shoot Catfoot strongly suggested he had killed before.

He speculated on what had happened on the journey out of Stainesville. It occurred to him that, despite his ploy, the girl might have recognized him when he was working his way through the cars in his search. By pure chance the man could have been elsewhere in the train, maybe using a water closet. On his return she had informed him of Catfoot's presence and he had taken to the roof of the car to avoid being seen, also to provide a way of getting the drop on the agent.

Eventually Catfoot stumbled away from the rails and took stock of the habitations at the side of the halt. Although small, at least it gave the appearance of an established town, the telegraph lines indicating it was civilized enough to be connected to the outside world.

'What the hell's happened to you?' the sheriff asked, when he made an appearance in the law office.

Catfoot explained, then asked, 'When's the next train?'

'Same time two days hence.'

Catfoot cursed. There was no point in acquiring a new horse and trying to pursue them at the moment. The animal wouldn't be able to keep up with a train, and he was too exhausted and bruised to ride. He had to reconcile himself to yet another hold-up and take up the pursuit by train in two days. He needed some way of delaying the renegades. The problem was he had nothing to connect Logan with the bank heist. As a worker with a private agency, albeit one that usually had the cooperation of public law officers, he needed firm evidence to get them actively involved in a case. He had an idea.

'I saw telegraph wires,' he said. 'Could you cable the law office in Tucumcari and get them to detain the pair when they arrive?'

'Ain't beyond the realms of possibility. The marshal out there might be obliging. What's this fellow's name?'

'Maybe Logan but don't know for sure. But I can give some description of him. The girl goes under the stage name of Gypsy Jane but she's probably travelling under a different moniker.'

'If you don't even know the guy's name, have you got enough on him to justify an arrest?'

'Yeah, personal assault. Back awhiles the bozo jumped me on the train.' He felt the back of his head where the woman had hit him. 'In fact, they can both be detained on that charge.'

'OK. You give me all the information you can and I'll put through a message. I know the officer out there — old Judd Brown — so he should cooperate.'

When the lawman had written down the details he looked up at his visitor and assessed the grazes. 'While I put this wire through you mosey over to the doc's and get those abrasions cleaned. You'll find his place a little way down the main drag.'

★   ★   ★

After he had been cleaned up, Catfoot booked a room and took a meal. Then he checked that the lawman had sent a message to his colleague in Tucumcari.

'Yeah,' the man said. 'Explained the situation. Gave your name and details. And got his reply here.' He pushed a piece of paper across his desk. 'Old Judd is an amenable sort. If those bozos turn up at Six Shooter Siding they'll be kept in Judd's slammer waiting on your arrival.'

'Thanks.'

'Now this ain't a regular halt but trains usually stop for water and wood. So leave it with me — I'll make sure it stops to pick you up. Hey, if you're lucky your ticket might still be valid.'

Catfoot nodded, hoping that his luck stretched to more than saving a few dollars on a train ticket. 'Much obliged, Sheriff.'

At the telegraph office he sent his own message to Denver, informing his boss that the case was firming up.

And it was still early in the evening when he eased his sore and aching body into bed.

★ ★ ★

It was late afternoon next day that he dropped down onto the sandy soil of

Tucumcari. With the hot New Mexico sun beating down he surveyed the small group of shacks and cluster of tents known as Six Shooter Siding.

Although being stuck in a train for such a long time was frustrating, the journey had allowed him to take some more much needed rest. But his frustration mounted when he got to the law office to collect his prisoners.

'Sorry, pal,' the marshal said. 'The parties have left town.'

'How come?'

The man looked sheepish. 'My deputy and I took the pair into custody as they debouched from the train. They protested their innocence of any crime but we wished to cooperate with your agency so they were incarcerated in our little jail here.' He nodded to the cell at the back of the building.

'And?'

'There's only me and my deputy. I'd retired for the night and left my assistant in charge. Apparently the woman kept complaining she was ill

— something about a women's ailment, she said. Shoot, he's just a young man and they took advantage of him. So when I turned up this morning he was bound and gagged, and the birds had flown.'

'Did you pursue them?'

'No. As I've said, there's only the two of us overworked critters here — we just don't have the resources.'

'Haven't you heard of a posse?'

'You don't seem to understand, Mr Catfoot. This is just a tent city. We don't stretch to committees and such that might organize fancy posses. Anyways, I was only incarcerating them as a favour to your company and had no charges of my own against them.'

'How did they leave?'

'There I can help you. We learned they bought horses from the local livery stable. There are also witnesses to their leaving town. Here, I'll show you.' He walked across to a map on the wall and placed a finger on it. 'See. They were seen heading out along this trail. That'll take them up into the Rockies.'

He went to the grimy window and pointed to a flattopped mesa. 'That's Tucumcari, some kind of place venerated by the Indians. It's that that gives this place its name. Your folk took the trail which passes it.'

Catfoot returned to the map and absorbed something of the geography of the region. 'Who's in charge of the livery?'

'Jerry Cord. Good feller; know him well. Used to be the blacksmith for a local cattle outfit that we worked for before we both settled in town. Had a portable forge that he toted on drives. Nothing he don't know about animals. In fact, ain't nothing he don't know about human doctoring. Used to be our doctor out on the range; pulled teeth and everything.'

'Where's his place?'

'A couple of blocks down the drag. Can't miss it. Only smithy in town.'

'Thanks.'

Minutes later Catfoot noted the sign

'J. Cord — Proprietor' over a building, and entered. The floor was straw-covered and there were several stalls. There was no one in evidence but he could hear clanking coming through the doorway to an adjoining area.

He passed through and found himself in a blacksmith's forge.

'Mr Cord?' he asked of the burly man clanging a hammer against a sliver of red-hot metal on an anvil.

The fellow hit the metal a few more times. 'Yeah.'

Catfoot introduced himself and the smith dropped the metal into a bucket of water. 'And?' he prompted as the thing sizzled.

Catfoot explained his circumstances and his meeting with the marshal.

'Yeah,' the man said, 'I heard later the couple had bust out of jail.' While he wiped his hands he carefully appraised his visitor. 'So you're a lawman after renegades?'

'Not exactly a lawman, but acting in that capacity with the endorsement and cooperation of the law. So I'd be obliged if you could give me some description of their horses.'

'No problem. The man's on a chestnut Tennessee. Big animal, over sixteen hands. The gal chose a Morgan; smaller, no more than fourteen hands.'

Catfoot nodded. 'Thanks. That could be useful. Now I need a horse, too.'

'Come on.'

The man took him outside to the corral holding several horses. He pointed to a bonnet-faced pinto. 'If you'll take my recommendation, that's the mount for you. You treat him right, he's got the stamina for a long haul. But he's got a streak of quarter in him that'll give you speed when you want it.'

'That's the one,' Catfoot said.

The smith took a rope and, despite his bulk, gracefully scaled the fence. Shortly he was handing over the horse to its new owner.

Catfoot stroked it, noting the blue eyes glinting in the sun and a bluish tinge where the light and dark patches met. 'We're gonna get on fine, pal.'

The smith sensed the immediate affinity between man and beast. 'I like to see my animals going to folk who'll appreciate them.' Then, 'Have you had much experience tracking, young man?'

'Well, I wouldn't say I was exactly Fennimore Cooper's Pathfinder, but I've done my share.'

'Good. Tell you why. Come back into the forge.'

Catfoot tied up his new horse and followed the man inside.

'When a horse goes lame,' the proprietor continued, 'provided it's not something drastic like a broken bone, a good blacksmith can correct it, if he knows how. See, you assess the precise nature of the lameness and you build a tailored shoe that helps to correct the fault while, at the same time, it encourages a natural healing of the lameness. A horse's body, like yours and mine and any other critter the good Lord created, has a capacity to heal itself.'

He noted the look in his listener's eyes that indicated he didn't understand the relevance.

'The point of this lecture,' he continued, 'is that the Tennessee that this feller bought had been lame and I had made such a shoe for it. It was successful and in time the thing improved. But it wasn't 100%. There was still a little lameness. It was so slight that most folk wouldn't even notice it — but I knew it wasn't quite right and it would be permanent. So I made another special shoe.'

He crossed to the wall and took down a shoe from a nail. 'Here, this was my first shot.' He pointed to metal that ran at an angle filling a section of the arc. 'See? The one the guy's horse is wearing is similar to this. You see a hoofprint like that in the dust and you'll know you've cut sign of the Tennessee.'

17

He rode for three days without seeing anyone. It was just the kind of territory he himself would make for if he were on the run.

The blacksmith's tell-tale clue was proving invaluable and Catfoot became adept at spotting it. Some times the progress of the couple was easy to follow. At other times he would have to slip from the saddle and look closely for tracks, scanning from side to side in a systematic way. When the runaways crossed rocky terrain leaving little trace, he would have to take a chance with a direction that looked feasible. If he cut no sign within a given distance he would backtrack and reconsider.

The region being so desolate he assumed that any horse droppings he came across marked their trail. On one occasion flies directed him to human manure. Such signs, no matter how vague, raised his spirits.

As long as there was daylight and sign to follow, he moved. Apart from short meal breaks he maintained his progress. He knew his own limits but not his horse's so, at times, he would proceed on foot to give his animal some respite.

Water was abundant in nature but by the fourth day, not having come across any habitation, he was out of provisions. It did not unduly concern him because it was wild country and he was aware of game, not abundant, but there were wild turkey and geese even the occasional antelope. He was at the point of considering doing some hunting when he came across a trapper. The man not only shared an evening meal of rabbit with him but in the morning supplied him breakfast and gave him some jerky for his journey.

★ ★ ★

On the fifth day his tiredness was getting to him when, following the trail into the mountains, he came to a clearing. The place marked the site of a deserted line shack. But more importantly, a couple of horses were tethered alongside — one large, one smaller.

He dropped from the saddle and retraced his steps into the thicket. He tied his horse out of sight to a tree. Cautiously he made his approach to the building. Closer, he could make out a chestnut Tennessee and a Morgan. *At long last he'd reached the end of his pursuit!*

He circled the building, keeping his distance, particularly from the horses, so he wouldn't be heard. There was a couple of windows, but each had sacking draped over it.

Problem now was how to get the drop on those inside. He had the element of surprise. But they could surprise him. There were only two horses but had they met someone there? Or maybe the shack had already been occupied when they arrived? Until he knew, he figured it would be foolhardy to simply crash his way in.

He was some distance from the building when the door suddenly opened and he saw the shape of a man — a big man — silhouetted against the light. A woman's voice came from inside and the man replied. Remaining in the doorway, the man continued the conversation while he guided a stream of urine onto the planking outside.

Catfoot couldn't make out the words but the exchange seemed casual enough. The door closed. His feeling was that the tone of the conversation suggested there were just the two of them. And the door looked flimsy, easy enough to bust through.

He was firming up his ideas in this direction and had crept up to the side of the building at the front with his gun in hand when the door opened again. This time it was the woman; and he recognized her as Gypsy Jane. She had a basin of water, the contents of which she flung to the ground.

As she was turning Catfoot sprinted forward and pushed the woman so that she sprawled back into the shack.

With his gun levelled, he had the drop on the man inside.

The man looked up, utter surprise in his eyes.

But Catfoot was equally surprised.

18

He has looking straight at a dead man. The man seated at a table with a mug of coffee and bathed in the light of an oil lamp was none other than Dick Bodeen himself.

'What the hell?' the man roared, heaving at the Beaumont-Adams in his holster.

But in a second, Catfoot was at his side with his own gun barrel jammed into Bodeen's throat. 'Let it go.'

He looked back at the girl who was getting to her feet. 'And no funny business, ma'am, or he gets it.'

He yanked Bodeen's gun from its holster and stepped back, indicating a vacant chair at the table. 'And you, ma'am, sit down.'

Keeping his gun levelled he walked to the door and kicked it shut.

'And who are you to come busting in

like that?' Bodeen wanted to know.

'Jim Catfoot of the Pinkerton Detective Agency.'

'I suppose you're the guy from the train?'

'Yeah. The one you jumped. And the one you set up at Queenie's place. That's another one I owe you for.'

'A Pinkie, eh?'

'Yeah.'

'And you've tailed us right up to here?' Bodeen said, then shook his head. 'And I thought I'd fooled you guys.'

'You did.'

'Then how come you're here?'

This wasn't the optimal time for talking so Catfoot didn't reply. For a while he stared at the man whom for so long he'd thought was dead. 'Bodeen, eh?' he said contemplatively. 'Huh.'

'Yeah. So, if you didn't figure it was me, how come you been trailing us?'

Catfoot thought on it. It still wasn't the time for talking but he needed some questions of his own answering so he obliged in the hope that he could get Bodeen to open up.

'OK,' he said as a preliminary. 'At the start I was just trying to get some background on you. Couldn't understand why you'd given your name during the train hold-up back up in Oregon; made no sense. Then as I started investigating I began to develop a hunch that there was a third guy in the bank hold-up. I was trailing you to try to prove the notion, but then, the way you began acting, like getting concerned about someone following you, not to mention paying someone to stop me, then throwing me off the train, told me there was something serious going on.'

'So what happens now?'

'Come morning, I'm taking the pair of you in.' He settled down on his haunches and turned to his own questions. 'Who was the guy they buried in your place?'

'That's for you to find out, Mr Investigator.'

'You're some tough *hombre*, I'll give you that — killing a couple of pals just to cover your tracks.'

Bodeen gave a dismissive gesture with his head.

'You had no qualms in shooting your long-time pardner?' Catfoot persisted.

'Billy Boy? No.' He shrugged and let out a loud breath. 'OK, he'd been with me some time and had proved useful. I acknowledge that — but he had to go. I don't kill unless absolutely necessary. Hey, I got some principles. Besides, killing ups the ante from the law side. There's a difference between star-packers chasing you for robbery and chasing you for murder. They kinda put in more effort, you know? Trouble was, Billy Boy had killed a guard during the train knock-over way up in Oregon. That meant that we'd go up a couple of pegs on the wanted list.

'So, to cover myself as best I could, I made sure *they* knew it wasn't me who killed the guard, and from that point on it was just a matter of time before I got rid of Billy Boy. It was the bozo's own fault. His ventilating that guard had turned him into a millstone round my neck. Then I saw how I could kill two birds with one stone, as they say. The act of getting him out of the way could actually help me in covering my tracks after the bank job. Putting a slug in him and dumping him in the river alongside my look-a-like would give the appearance that we'd had a disputation over the loot and that we'd put each other down in a shoot-out. Seemed to me — if I could work the right strings — there was a high chance the investigators would go for the story.'

Catfoot stifled a yawn and hoped his captive didn't notice the widening of his eyes as he fought to keep them open. 'Yeah, the look-a-like. Everybody who looked at that stiff thought it was you. How the hell did you get yourself a carbon copy like that?'

'Didn't think he was such a look-a-like that you could call him a carbon copy. For a start, I reckon I'm a mite purtier, don't you think?'

Catfoot ignored the banter. 'He was sure close enough to pass for your picture on a dodger.'

'Yeah, that's what I figured.'

Catfoot mused on it. 'A daguerreotype is crude at best. And a man's features are different in death. I suppose that any differences might be obscured by such a comparison. Plus, folk often tend to see what they expect to see. So, this look-a-like — or near look-a-like — was it Big Jake Logan?'

'Hell, no. Ain't seen Jake for a coon's age.'

'So, who was it?'

'Some guy I happened on.'

'Happened on? How did you come across him?'

'Pure chance, my friend. It fell this way. Me and Billy Boy wus relaxing one evening in a saloon. There was a half-decent game of poker in progress. We got ourselves invited in but Billy Boy was as lunkhead as ever and soon blew his change. While he was out taking a leak I won a couple of good hands. That was too much for the penny-ante hicks I was playing so the game folded and I went back to the bar to get myself some refreshment. When Billy Boy returned from the privy he noticed the game was over and looked around the gathering for me. I was waving to get his attention but he didn't see me through the crowd. Instead, the bozo staggered across to the other end of the bar and put his arms round the shoulders of a complete stranger. 'Howdy-do, Dick,' Billy Boy says. 'Make enough dough to buy your old pardner another drink?' Hah!'

Bodeen continued chuckling at the recollection for a moment. 'Hell, this stranger looks him up and down, pushes him away like he's dog filth. 'Git your hands off me, you rum-pot, unless you want to lose a few teeth. I don't knows you from Adam.' Billy, he steps back, looking the guy over with those stupid, empty eyes of his. 'Gee, am I sorry, mister,' he says. 'I thought you was — ' This guy pushes him further away and says, 'Well, as you can see, I ain't so get lost.' When I studied the guy I could understand Billy Boy's confusion.'

He gestured to his features. 'He'd got the same kinda square face that's been looking back at me from the mirror for years. Even got a droop moustache. Similar build too. Hell, you didn't have to have a gutful of booze to make the error. You could make the mistake if you didn't know me too well.' He chuckled. 'Like if you only knew me from reward posters for example.'

His tone took on a swagger as he continued. 'Only took me a minute thinkifying to see how the bozo could be the answer to my problems — if I could fix it for him to die in my place while making sure there was enough of my trappings around to complete the picture.'

'And how did you talk him into following the owlhoot trail?'

'That wasn't difficult. Got jawing.

Rowdy his name was. Found out he had about as much brains as Billy Boy. Fitted the bill in other ways too, being a no-account drifter. All I had to do was promise him the moon, tell him how important he would be in our little band and slip him a few dollars in the meantimes. A perfect plan.'

Bodeen studied Catfoot for a moment. 'Tell me, how come I didn't sucker you?'

'I've told you, you did. And for a spell you even suckered us into believing the money had been washed down the Arkansas. There was only one fault in your perfect plan. You were too greedy. If your main aim had been to fake your own death, you should have left it at that and said goodbye to the loot. See, if you'd let us recoup all the money we would have likely hightailed it back to headquarters and closed the file. However, our needing to put some effort into looking for it gave me time to think. As it fell, it tied in with me having personal reasons for needing a break, so I used the opportunity to do a little more investigating. But all I was trying to do was get a little more background on you. I tell you, Bodeen, until we came face to face just now it had never occurred to me that you might still be alive.'

The girl rose and crossed the room to a blanket carelessly strewn on the floor.

'Hey, what you doing?' Catfoot snapped, looking at her but keeping his gun on Bodeen.

'You guys seem to have a lot to talk about. I don't know about the pair of you but it's been a long day and I'm going to grab myself some shuteye.' She picked up the blanket and investigated it with some disdain. 'If you two are going to jawbone all night, keep your voices down.'

'I'm watching you, ma'am,' Catfoot said.

She turned to face them and began shaking dust from the blanket. 'Watch all you like, feller. You ain't gonna see nothing.'

He still kept his eye on her.

'Jeez,' she said as dust billowed out with each flick. She coughed and leaned back her head while extending the blanket even further in front of her. Suddenly she lunged forward and flipped the thing clear over the oil lamp, knocking it over.

There was a crash in the ensuing darkness as Bodeen's chair went over.

Before he knew it, Catfoot found himself grappling with the big man in the blackness. Bodeen soon had Catfoot on the floor. 'Light the lamp!' he yelled.

The two continued scuffling and Catfoot felt an increasingly familiar fist wham against his chin.

When the lamp resumed its flicker, Bodeen leapt back and Catfoot looked up to see the gun in the big man's hand.

19

'Quick thinking, gal,' Bodeen said as he lined up the barrel on the prostrate man's torso. The light falling on the gunman's face showed a carved expression of evil intent. His finger was tightening on the trigger and the distance between the two men was too great for Catfoot to do anything about it.

'No, Dick!' the girl shouted. 'Don't do it.'

Bodeen glanced at the woman as she added, 'It could be real bad for us if you killed him.'

Her words had the effect of nudging him into thinking things through. 'Just don't move,' he said to Catfoot, as he righted the chair and dropped his bulk on it.

He thought some more then said, 'Tell you what, Pinkie. I'm gonna give you a choice. At the end of the day your company wants to retrieve its client's money. That's what it's in business for. So this is your choice. You promise to let me and the woman go, I'll show you where the money is and take some of it to tide me over, enough to see us through a season, say a grand.'

'A grand?' Gypsy Jane mouthed. 'After what we've been through?'

'You don't understand, woman,' Bodeen said. 'I'm offering a deal here. This guy would have to go back with most of the haul to satisfy his bosses. All we need is travelling money.'

The woman grunted. 'And you'd trust him? Are you crazy? He's a lawman.'

Bodeen studied Catfoot's eyes. 'Yeah, I'd take his word. I think he's that kind of feller, a real old-fashioned straight shooter. Ain't many of 'em left. Besides he ain't a lawman. He works for a private company and, like I said, their main priority is looking after their client's money. Sure they like to bring folks like me to justice — they got that much of the 'law' in their veins — but if it's a cold choice between justice and retrieving stolen goods, they go for the goods. Law comes second. Ain't I right, Pinkie?'

'Mebbe.'

'They'd be on the lookout for me all right. But as I hadn't killed their man and had let them have most of the dough back I reckon, in the circumstances, they wouldn't put all their resources into the chase and the heat would die down pretty quick. Any faults with my logic, Pinkie?'

'And what if I don't accept your offer?'

A humourless smile stretched Bodeen's lips and he grunted. 'I kinda hope you don't. That way I come out the better. I kill you and get clear with all of it.'

'You know what that would mean.'

'Yeah, but with you forcing me into it, it'd be a chance I'd be prepared to take,'

'You could just knock him out and tie him up,' the woman suggested.

'Talk sense, woman. Soon as he was out of it he'd be on our trail and we'd be back to the starting line.'

'OK, you could just wound him so he can't chase us.'

'You don't know the Pinkies. Once he got back with the tale about me getting way with the loot and putting a hole in one of their agents, they'd never let up.' He rearranged his posture a little without taking his eyes off his prisoner. 'You told your bosses you think I might still be breathing?'

'That's for you to ponder on.'

Bodeen thought about it. 'No, you've already said the possibility hadn't occurred to you so you won't have told them anything. But that don't alter the proposition. If I kill you and take all the loot, it's likely they're gonna work things out eventually and then I'm gonna be looking over my shoulder for the rest of my days. I know that much about your outfit. On the other hand, I let you go, you'll tell 'em it ain't me back in that coffin. But then I'll be clear of the territory and, like I've said, in time the pressure will be off.'

'As we're putting up choices, there's a third alternative,' Catfoot said.

'And what's that?'

'You got the jump on me because I'm tired. But you're just as tired. And you're still recovering from emptying out your insides after Queenie's cooking. On top of that, the riding has drained your body, and you'll find you need to sleep a lot sooner than normal. Then I take advantage of your attention wavering.'

'Yeah. That could happen. But the moment I start to feel drowsy I'll give you the choice one last time. You refuse and you force me to cut my losses, get it over with, put a bullet into you and take my chances.'

Catfoot pondered for a moment. He knew Bodeen meant it. At least he could try stalling. 'OK, it's a deal. You take a grand and we'll do as you say. I'm a practical man. It's not my money — but it's my life.'

Bodeen drew himself up. 'Now you're talking sense. Right, that's settled. And you don't spill the beans on me to any lawman on the way back — or organize any action against me. What you say and do when you finally get back to the Pinkie headquarters is your business.'

'Agreed.'

'By then I'll be living who-knows-where under a different name.'

'And you'll be taking up the owlhoot trail again?'

Bodeen chuckled. 'Now that'll be for *you* to ponder on.'

'If you don't, that'll be the first time I've heard of a leopard changing its spots.'

'S'pose it would. Hell, I'm giving up a lot here and we got expensive tastes, ain't we, Gypsy? A feller's gotta make a living somehow. You must allow me that, Pinkie. OK?'

'OK. None of my business, unless you catch the eye of my bosses again.'

After a while Bodeen slipped his gun

into its holster. 'No need for that now we're all old pals.'

'You sure you can trust him?' the girl said.

'Whatever he is, he's a man of his word, ain't you, Pinkie? OK, let's get moving.' He gestured to the door. 'Outside. The dough's cached not too far from here.'

Catfoot moved towards the door, turning his back on the outlaw. On this matter, he trusted the other, too.

But trust was not enough. There are other things in this world that can be more important and can override matters. Such as the butt end of a revolver which came crashing down on Catfoot's skull as he moved through the doorway.

20

The man who had posed as a drummer calling himself Chauncey Goodman moved quickly through the doorway. Inside, his first action was to put a slug into Bodeen's shoulder that sent him caroming backwards to the wooden boards.

Gypsy Jane screamed and ran at the intruder. She managed to claw her nails across his face before he whopped her with the gun so that she, too, crumpled to the floor.

The erstwhile drummer crossed the room and yanked the gun from Bodeen's holster. He stepped back, checked the Pinkerton man was still out, then turned to eye the other fallen man. 'You suffering, Bodeen?'

Bodeen pulled his hand away from his shoulder and saw the blood. 'Of course, I'm suffering, you pissant.'

'Good.'

On hands and knees, Gypsy worked her way across the floor and tried to examine her man's wound.

'Don't pull any tricks, ma'am,' the man warned.

Bodeen screwed up his face while Gypsy did her exploring, then he looked back at his attacker. 'What the hell's going on, O'Hara?'

★ ★ ★

'Hey, watch your cussing in front of a lady.'

'I ain't no goddamn lady, you imbecile,' Gypsy said as she did her tending.

'I was being ironic, ma'am.'

'You talk like you know the bastard, Dick,' the girl said.

'Yeah,' Bodeen snarled. 'What the hell you doing here, O'Hara?'

'You might well ask, pal.'

'I am asking.'

O'Hara threw a glance back to check

that Catfoot was still immobile. 'Heard you and my brother was dead. Like everybody, I thought you and he'd had a disputation over the loot from the Ogden bank heist and had ended up shooting each other. Billy Boy and I were never close but he was kin and for what you did to my kid brother you needed a bullet in your black heart, and I was the one to do it. Trouble was, as far as I knew you'd already been eliminated. So, me paying you back wasn't possible. I couldn't kill a dead man. Fate had done the job for me. What they call irony.'

He looked at the woman. 'There's that word 'irony' again, ma'am.'

'Damn you, you sneaky bastard.' she hissed. 'You wouldn't have gunned down my Bodeen in a fair showdown.'

He chuckled and continued. 'And that was the end of that until I heard there was a Pinkerton agent asking questions about you. That intrigued me — why was he asking questions about a dead man?'

'This wound needs cleaning,' the woman interrupted.

'No it don't, ma'am. He's due for worse.'

She ignored him and crossed to collect a pitcher of water from the table.

O'Hara watched her as he continued. 'So I made my own enquiries and found there had been a third guy in the hold-up. Then everything pointed to *him* having killed you and my brother. That's what the Pinkie thought too and that's why he was on his trail. My learning that there was a third man meant that Billy Boy's murder still needed *somebody* paying the price. How could I track down this mysterious bozo? Well, ain't never heard of the Pinks losing a man yet, so I figured my best bet was to follow him. But I had to do it in some clandestine fashion. Got myself a case full of garbage and made out I was a no-account drummer. That way, if he spotted me anytime during his travels he would be less likely to be suspicious.'

'I need a handkerchief from my bag,' the woman interjected.

'Stay where you are,' Billy Boy's brother snapped.

Again she ignored him and fetched her bag which she took to Bodeen's side.

O'Hara resumed. 'So here we are. And it's payback time. Out of the way, lady.'

'You can have the booty,' Bodeen said weakly. 'It's out there. It's all yours.'

'I ain't here for loot. Now, like I said, out of the way, lady.'

In her nursing activity, Gypsy Jane had momentarily obscured her man. And when she did finally move as O'Hara instructed, the derringer from her bag was in Bodeen's hand.

And firing.

The drummer's gun thundered its own response.

★　★　★

The din kick-started Catfoot's brain back to life and his eyes sprang open.

Unaware for a second of where he was or what had happened, it was pure instinct that caused him to start rolling across the dirt. But when he came to his feet he knew exactly where he was. He glanced around, looking for something to use as a weapon, and found a chunk of wood.

He leapt to the door, flattening himself against the side. Hefting the chunk of wood, he cautiously investigated. There were two crumpled men on the floor and a lot of blood. It didn't matter how it had actually happened; it was clear they were both dead. Gypsy was whimpering over the still form of Bodeen.

Catfoot could make out her saying, 'Twice I've mourned for the man.'

'If you *are* mourning him, ma'am, it's for the first time,' he said, as he moved in and surveyed the scene. 'But I gotta give it to you. You were a darn fast thinker, giving me that grief stuff back in Dodge when I told you he was dead — and you knew he was still breathing God's good air.'

He studied the other man's features. 'I've seen this guy before. Who is he?'

'The bastard is Billy O'Hara's brother.'

'On the revenge trail, eh?'

'Yeah, he was following you, hoping you would lead him to whoever killed Billy Boy. And you did.'

Then Catfoot remembered the man from the stagecoach. 'He's a good actor. I'd tagged him as a no-account drummer.' He looked back at the woman. 'You're a good actress, too, ma'am. You sure had me fooled. A performance worthy of your profession as an artiste.'

'Well, the tears are real this time, Mr Smarty Pants.'

By the time he had collected the guns, she was on her feet, wiping away the vestige of wetness from her cheeks.

'Well, if that's the truth, ma'am,' he said, 'I'm right sorry it had to happen this way.'

She sighed. 'Ain't no use in crying over spilt milk.' She was suddenly composed in voice and demeanour, displaying recognition that something was over and it was time to move on. 'Huh, this was supposed to be the big one. The one that was gonna set us up — but it was nothing but a pipe dream. I figure, at the end of the day, the man would always be trouble.'

Catfoot broke into her thoughts. 'If you're up to it, ma'am, show me where the cash is.'

'You think I would?'

'Yes, ma'am. If you don't, I'm gonna tie you up and start looking. I know the money's close by but you could get hungry while I'm looking. No to mention the mess you'll get into not being able to attend to relieving yourself in a civilized fashion. Then if I still don't find it I'm gonna take you into town. By then you'll be a real stink. I'll telegraph the agency, they'll send out a team and the loot will be found. So, you'll save yourself a deal of trouble if . . . '

'Yeah, I get the picture. Come on then.'

21

'And what happens to me?' she asked. 'I didn't do no robbing or killing.'

She'd taken him to where the money was hidden beneath some thick vegetation. After counting it he had tied the two bodies to their horses and was now preparing the remaining horses for departure.

'You're an accessory, ma'am. That makes you culpable. You've got to be taken in.'

She snuggled up to him. 'Your bosses don't know about the money. They still think it's been washed down the river. What about you and me becoming a twosome and using the dough to set up house together?'

'The dough's going back.'

'Is there nothing I can do or say to make you change you mind?'

'No, ma'am. All the options got

talked through back in the cabin.'

'One option didn't,' she said coquett- ishly and began undoing the front of her clothing. He glanced at her and grunted. 'That'll get you nowhere. Cover yourself up decent, ma'am.'

'You don't find me attractive?' she said, as she fondled her exposed breasts.

He was a man deprived of a woman's touch for a long time. But he was also a determined man with a sense of duty. 'Like I said, get your clothes back on.'

She paused, reflected on the resolu- tion in his voice, then she began doing up her buttons. 'Huh, more of a gentleman than even Bodeen imagined. All I can say is: no pleasing some guys.'

★   ★   ★

The light of the next day was already getting a grip when they set out. Come nightfall they made camp and took a meal.

After a few mouthfuls he looked at

241

her. 'I've been thinking. I've been going over what happened back there in the cabin and I've remembered you making some attempt to quash Bodeen's ideas about killing me.'

He rubbed the back of his head in recollection. 'That was some strong-arm slam you gave me back on that train but, no denying, the notion of you trying to stop Bodeen shooting me keeps coming back. It was clear he'd got half a mind to plug me. I suppose I gotta be grateful to you for that. Your intervention means you ain't all hard-nosed woman. You got some compassion.'

'Yeah, compassion, that's the word. That must count for something, don't it?'

'That's what I'm saying, ma'am. I reckon it does.'

'So?'

He thought about it some more. 'Tell you what I'll do. When we hit town I'll give you the thousand Bodeen was marking out for himself in the deal we were fixing before O'Hara's brother bust in. Before circumstances changed I'd already agreed to that. Bodeen was right: as far as the company's concerned, they're gonna be glad to get the bulk of the dough back. As it is, there's already some money missing so they won't miss a few more bills. So, I'll let you have the grand, then you light out and I don't mention you in my report.'

'You'd do that?'

He nodded. 'Yeah. In my small way I try to deal straight with folks, and I figure I gotta make some recompense for the little bit of concern for me you showed back in that cabin. But I don't want to see or hear of you again. If you can't keep your nose clean, ma'am, try to keep out of my bailiwick.'

'You know, you ain't such a bad guy after all. What's your first name'?'

'Jim.'

'Thanks, Jim.'

The rest of the meal continued in relative silence. While they were taking coffee Catfoot built a smoke and handed it to her.

She took it and rolled it contemplatively between her fingers. She lay back on the grass and watched him fiddle with the makings of his own cigarette. 'The offer is still open,' she said softly.

'What offer's that?' he asked as he licked the paper to complete the cigarette.

She smiled suggestively. 'You know, back there.'

It took him a second to make the link. 'Oh, the goods you were laying out on the table a whiles back.'

She carefully laid down the cigarette and undid her buttons, displaying her charms again. 'It wouldn't be part of any deal, you understand. Just some late night relaxation by an evening fire.'

He felt himself stiffening, the first time in a while. 'Must say, I wouldn't say no to some relaxation on a warm evening. But — like somebody once told me — no strings?'

'No strings. On the other hand if you were to add a thousand bucks to my leaving present, I wouldn't argue.'

'A thousand?' His eyes roamed over

the exposed flesh. 'What the hell, it ain't my money.'

He moved towards her and began to loosen his clothes. 'You know there ain't many perquisites in this job.'

'Perquisites — what's one of them?'

'Perquisite, it's a ten-dollar word for side benefit. Hard riding not to mention regular whuppings — and all a feller gets at the end of the day is a pay-packet and a few dollars by way of bonus once in a blue moon.'

She looked momentarily contrite. 'I'm real sorry I added to your bruises back on the train. But you were giving my man a helluva thumping.'

'Forget it. All in a day's work.'

She smiled and lay back, now completely naked in the warm evening air with arms outstretched and welcoming. 'Enough talking, Mr Pinkie. Just be my guest.'

He eased himself beside her.

And settled down to enjoy a rare perquisite.

We do hope that you have enjoyed reading this large print book.

Did you know that all of our titles are available for purchase?

We publish a wide range of high quality large print books including:
Romances, Mysteries, Classics
General Fiction
Non Fiction and Westerns

Special interest titles available in large print are:
The Little Oxford Dictionary
Music Book, Song Book
Hymn Book, Service Book

Also available from us courtesy of Oxford University Press:
Young Readers' Dictionary
(large print edition)
Young Readers' Thesaurus
(large print edition)

For further information or a free brochure, please contact us at:
Ulverscroft Large Print Books Ltd.,
The Green, Bradgate Road, Anstey,
Leicester, LE7 7FU, England.
Tel: (00 44) **0116 236 4325**
Fax: (00 44) **0116 234 0205**

Other titles in the
Linford Western Library:

HIGH STAKES AT CASA GRANDE

T. M. Dolan

A gambler down on his luck, Latigo arrives in town bent on vengeance. His aim is to ruin Major Lonroy Crogan, the owner of the town of Casa Grande, and then to kill him. With a loaned poker stake, he soon makes enough money to threaten Crogan's empire by buying up property. However, danger lurks on the horizon and Latigo's plans seem doomed to failure. Will he be forced to flee Casa Grande as an all round loser?

SHOWDOWN AT TRINIDAD

Daniel Rockfern

The big man knew that with no one left who could connect him with the train robbery, he was almost clear. No one, that is, except Frank Angel, special investigator for the US Justice Department. And Hainin realised that there was no stopping the lawman's pursuit. He might get away clear with the money, but Angel would never quit looking for him . . . never forget. It was a pity. But if Hainin was to ever know peace, Angel had to die!